Groom Lake

By

Sarah E. England

ISBN: 979-8-8394-5071-4

1st Edition
www.sarahenglandauthor.co.uk

DARK FICTION BY SARAH E. ENGLAND

ABOUT THE AUTHOR

Sarah England is a UK author. At the fore of Sarah's body of work is the bestselling occult horror trilogy *Father of Lies, Tanners Dell,* and *Magda*, followed by *The Owlmen*. Stand-alone novels include *The Soprano, Hidden Company, Monkspike, Baba Lenka, Masquerade* and *Caduceus. The Witching Hour* is a collection of short stories; and *Groom Lake* is her latest book.

If you would like to be informed about future releases, there is a newsletter sign-up on Sarah's website. Please feel free to get in touch – it would be great to hear from you!

https://www.sarahenglandauthor.co.uk

PROLOGUE

GROOM LAKE, THE WELSH MARCHLANDS

BENEATH THE hard, pale blue of an October evening sky, the ruins of Woodsay Castle stood like broken soldiers on the peak of the hill, and a bleak wind whined around the stones from a time long past. Where an imposing fortress had once lorded over the valley below, only the grand arch of a doorway now remained, along with a few jagged walls and a derelict watchtower. In steadfast stillness they took the brunt of all weathers, skeletal silhouettes against the rose gold of a setting sun.

Out of breath, Lauren paused half way up the ascent and looked down. Shadows of dusk were already sweeping across the lowlands, the gilt-edged peaks of distant mountains ablaze as the fire of dying glory threw the whole valley into contrasting gloom. The trek had been far more arduous than she'd initially envisaged - the steep drop below pebble-dashed with fallen scree, Groom Lake Village now hidden from view. Stupid to have set out so late in the day! She squinted upwards. What to do? Nine Rings Hill had proved deceptive - it just hadn't looked this high standing at the bottom.

The sweat was drying quickly on her skin and a raw

chill shivered into her bones. She looked at her watch. Well, there was no point in coming all this way not to make it to the top. An owl screeched from a forest already dark, the only other sounds the rush of the wind and her own heartbeat. Hopefully the light would hold.

Without further inner discussion, she continued upwards, focusing on scaling the enormous terraces, which rose in tiers like a wedding cake. In between the rings there was a walk on the flat, before the next precipitous slope, each one exhausting to climb. On what she hoped was the last one but realised probably wasn't, there appeared a rocky outcrop known as The Skullcaps. She glanced across at the gravity-defying tumble of rocks clinging to the side of the hill, as if caught mid-fall to rest in the palm of an invisible hand. It was an extraordinary sight and, gasping for breath, she lingered.

What a strange, magical place this was, quite otherworldly. A couple of spidery trees had cleaved to the barren earth nearby, roots exposed like giant claws, the branches ghostly arms reaching into the void. How the wind whistled up here, she thought, blowing through those broken castle walls bleak and shrill. A wild imagination could almost convince itself there were voices calling…

She looked up. Not much further to go now. Eight rings down, one to go. And the journey thankfully now gained momentum as the flat areas shortened and the tip was neared. Nine Rings Hill was on odd phenomenon. Indeed, and this was hearsay, a secret whispered, but it was said that the kings of old had adopted the location as one of the most sacred in the world. If not *the* most sacred. Worth fighting for. Such was the legend, the myth.

Yet here it stood in abandoned silence.

On at long last reaching the summit, Lauren slumped to the ground and rolled onto her back. Everything hurt. Whatever had she been thinking on this, her first night here? And what about getting down again?

Oh, God…Lauren…Lauren…why do you do this to yourself? Mistake after mistake after mistake…

The fatigue was overwhelming, the outer world a blur, her legs as heavy as concrete as she lay panting; and just for a moment closed her eyes.

What happened then was like passing through a fine veil of mist, catching her totally off-guard. One moment the earth was stony and firm beneath her back, the next it began to pitch and roll like a wave, and she jerked sharply awake.

What the…?

Her breath hitched uncomfortably in her chest as she lay motionless. Had it been an earth tremor? But something fundamental had altered. The atmosphere had thickened and the shrieking wind had dropped to an unearthly moan. Alarmed, she sat up and looked around.

This was odd. Although the ground was still hard and cold, the tufts of hardy grass real beneath her palms, there was nothing to see now save a blinding whiteness, a kind of clean transcendent pain that spliced the heart.

Was this death? Did it happen so seamlessly?

Automatically she put a hand to her chest. The sounds on the wind had become the voices she'd fancied hearing earlier…Men, she realised…a battle cry stampeding through the aeons of time…and it was gaining momentum…

The unearthly roar was then upon her so quickly there was no time to register what was happening. The final moments of a deadly massacre had been caught and trapped in the very fabric of the weather-beaten stones and blood-soaked dirt, crystallised in one atom for all eternity. And the memory of it howled like banshees in the wind, rushing straight at her in a monumental astral sigh.

At the moment of impact, as her conscious mind met the trauma head on, a rapid succession of images was projected into her mind. And she saw, in that shard of clarity, that the men who were charging directly into glinting swords, whose horses screamed and reared, no longer inhabited the bodies that raced towards certain death. Perhaps the horror was too much to bear, but on both sides there were souls floating away like party balloons into the blue, blue dawn. And the memories of lives lived all too briefly passed through her as if they were her own, not of hatred, war and the lust for power, but of love – the embrace of a woman, or the downy head of a child – and regret, sadness, and shock! A sudden snap of understanding: what were they doing here? Over. Life was over, and it was far, far too late to turn back.

The moment lasted mere seconds.

Or had it?

When she came to, it was to find a crescent moon floating on the horizon. But how could that be? A solitary dog fox barked from across the valley, the distant spikes of pine trees now merging with the sky in a watercolour blur. How empty and eerie the place was - somehow static, caught in time. What a strange, strange thing! She'd never known anything like it. The air was so very cold, too - freezing in fact – like the depths of winter. Her heart bumped uncomfortably as she was forced to accept what lay before her eyes: the scene had changed dramatically, to one of newly dropped snow, and a night that was clear and glistening.

A faint noise, a swish of cloth, caused her to start and swing around.

What on earth…?

A line of figures in deeply-hooded robes barely distinguishable from the darkness had emerged from the gloom. They carried no lights, but instead a small bowl each, silently filing past the ruined castle walls, so close the waft of their garments fanned her skin. Her heart was hammering as she sat perfectly still, transfixed. Had they seen her? Was it some kind of ceremony?

It was only after the figures had glided past that comprehension slowly dawned. They were ghosts! Ghosts now blending with the watchtower, before stepping clean off the top of the hill, and vanishing into the night sky.

Confused, she shook her head, blinked repeatedly and told herself it wasn't real. The temperature had risen again and the sharp wind was back. It had either been a waking dream or the place was haunted. But where had they gone? She stood up. Was there something over the side? Torn between wanting to get back to the rented cottage before it got too dark and the desire to see over the edge, she hesitated for a moment, and then grabbed her rucksack. Pulling out her jacket she slipped it on and picked her way through the ancient earthworks towards the watchtower.

A gust of wind blasted back her hair as she surveyed the void below. And all further questions died on her lips. There was a line of steps leading down a sheer precipice into what appeared to be the gaping jaws of a cave.

Lauren stepped back.

The velvet cloak of night had now settled, the valleys

below a silent coal-black canopy of trees. Time to go. Another fox barked, followed by the ke-wick, ke-wick of a tawny owl, and rain now misted the air. More than that, though, far more – was the creeping shiver of unease spreading rapidly across her back.

Walking smartly back to where she'd left the rucksack, she picked it up, flicked on the torch and was already heading towards the downwards slope, when the whistle of the wind changed to a low growl. All the fine hairs on her neck and arms prickled.

Don't turn round…

But she couldn't help it. The feeling of a watchful presence rushing up behind her was overwhelming and she whipped around in self-defence. The orb of the torch bobbed in the darkness. There was no one there. Not a person. But there was…*something*…

She frowned, trying to make sense of what she was seeing. Not a man, no. Was it a cloud? A huge mass of blackness seemed to be rolling towards her.

Without further hesitation she clicked the rucksack into place and hurried towards the path.

***

Part One

Ephesians 6:12

'For we wrestle not against flesh and blood, but against principalities, against powers, against the rulers of the darkness of this world, against spiritual wickedness in high places.'

CHAPTER ONE
Groom Lake Village

Later that night Lauren lay in bed watching candlelight leap around the bedroom walls. How come the flames blew around in such an erratic dance when the room was as still and cold as a church crypt? The intense chill had set her bones to ice; one which the damp blankets did little to ease. She grimaced.

Thanks, Glynis!

It had taken nearly three hours to get back from Nine Rings Hill. This kind of countryside – with valleys flanked by densely forested slopes, lanes awash with running water, and no houses or streetlights – was tar black at night, with the torch lighting only a few feet ahead. Solid drizzle had added to the difficulty as she'd made her way downhill, before retracing the forest path to the lane and then the cottage.

And the sense of being watched had persisted. The presence had dogged her, an unwanted shadow, and every so often she'd stopped and turned, convinced someone was about to step out from the darkness of the trees. Despite the fresh scent of pine and fertile earth, the air was clogged and heavy, the rise and fall of her own breathing as loud as her heartbeat. The forest had a music all its own, with the rain spattering the canopy and the trickle of hidden streams hypnotic. So much water…had there ever been a place more sodden than here?

She saw herself as she must have looked from above - a reed-thin figure walking along a lane coursing with water that was ankle deep. Rain dripped from her long pale hair and ran down her face, one cold wet hand holding the torch, the other thrust into a pocket, the only sound the steady thud of boots on tarmac. There were no houses in sight and not a single car had passed, despite there being many road-kills - four maybe five pheasants, a bundle of bloody fur, and the remains of a rabbit. At one point, as she squinted into the rain, she thought an old man was walking towards her. Stooped, wearing a long mac and hat, he was picking his way along the lane with the aid of a stick. But as they drew closer he vanished into the scenery, a phantom in rainfall that by the time the cottage came into view, had become a downpour.

Now, shivering uncontrollably, she reached for her overcoat and piled it on top of the bed. Everything smelled of mould and damp. It spotted the corners of the walls and the backs of the curtains, the musty odour clinging to carpets and furniture. The only creatures that could thrive in here, she thought, were rodents and beetles. In fact, Clingbine Cottage looked as if it hadn't been inhabited in decades. How for shame could anyone have rented this out? She was trying not to cry. This was supposed to have been a respite from all that had happened, not to make matters worse; and she hardly had any money left!

Situated by the back gates of D'Avranches Grange Estate, she guessed it had once been used by estate workers and now served as a modest additional income for the farmer, or his wife anyway. 'Great walks and a secluded location,' had headed the advertisement - 'A perfect hideaway'. Well, that would be true! Any abode more hidden than this would be difficult to imagine.

She sighed, flexing her feet to keep the blood circulating. She hadn't been as frozen as this since childhood, although that must be such a distant memory she couldn't recall the circumstances, only that once she'd lost the sensation in her toes.

Tyler Moody's farm was about half a mile away in the direction of Owlbury, the nearest town, and it was his wife, Glynis, who'd shown her round that morning – a lifetime ago already.

After counting out Lauren's cash in the driveway, Glynis had pushed open the front door. "Here's your key, then. I'll just quickly show you where everything is."

A rush of stale air had met them in what was a small kitchen with a linoleum floor. There was a stand-alone cooker, a row of lime green cupboards with frosted glass doors, and a sink with a flowery curtain underneath.

Glynis flicked a switch and a bare overhead lightbulb slowly built up to a sulphur glow. Candles would be preferable to that, Lauren decided. "Cups and plates and such are in here. Pans in there…boiler's through here…"

Lost for words, Lauren barely heard anymore as she took in the peeling flocked wallpaper in the bedroom, and the gigantic spider in a bath tub stained with mustard tidemarks. No shower. The bed was a lumpy double, low to the floor, and apart from a bedside table, had no other furniture unless a clothes rail separated from the room by another curtain could be counted. And that was it: a single, ground floor dwelling no bigger than a cut-price motel room. Hardly the described country cottage! No wonder it had been cheap.

'Not cheap enough,' Lauren thought. And Glynis,

who'd snapped two weeks' worth into her handbag, did not look the type to hand it back.

As she'd stood at the entrance to the bedroom trying to quash a wave of despair, she heard Glynis swear loudly from the vicinity of the bathroom.

"Looks like we'll have to get the boiler fixed for you," she said.

"Doesn't it work?"

"No, I just said!" She glared at Lauren as if she had a frontal lobe missing. "I'll get Tyler to come and look at it tomorrow. Too late now. Anyway, is there anything else only I've to get back?"

"So, no hot water?"

"Not today, no."

"Is there a washing machine?"

"This is only a holiday cottage, isn't it? You'd have to go into Owlbury for that."

Glynis' accent was a soft-lilting Welsh, but delivered with clipped aggression. Her hair was steel grey, cut short over the ears, and she wore leggings and a multi-coloured, patchwork anorak. Lauren guessed her to be around fifty, but she'd probably looked the same for at least twenty years and would for the next.

"Anything else?"
"Just where to get bread and milk. Is there a shop?"

"In Owlbury."

"Nothing in Groom Lake? That I could walk to?"

Glynis turned to go. "No. Anyhow, I'm busy this afternoon so we'll see you tomorrow, all right?"

Fortunately there'd been a shop on the main road leading into the small market town so the trip was quick. She'd picked up some cheap crockery, cutlery and tea towels in addition to cleaning materials and basic food items, and by early afternoon the place was thoroughly scrubbed. Only then had she slumped onto the armchair in the kitchen.

Rain was beginning to sprinkle against the window pane, autumn leaves rustling around the door. What kind of bloody atrocious luck was this? As soon as she'd turned the car into the drive and seen the hollow-eyed cottage with its sagging moss-covered roof and peeling paintwork, her spirits had plunged. Behind it, wire netting separated a mud garden from a wooded area of telegraph pole pines, incongruous in an otherwise lushly sylvan valley, the cavernous interior tomb grey. There was an unworldly presence here that watched and unnerved, the silence lifeless, the air icily damp; and she'd felt it the moment she'd arrived.

Lying in bed now as the rain intensified, and water poured off guttering into pools of already sodden earth, she acknowledged a lingering resentment at having had to clean up someone else's grime, and having to lie here racked with cold. Glynis Moody had a brass neck renting this out without cleaning it or making sure the heating worked. At least it was cheap, she supposed, and how else could she have afforded a couple of much-needed weeks away from the stress and worry of her life? No, she would enjoy it – get this sorted out and then think carefully about where to go and what to do next. The answers lay here she was certain, in the peace and solitude of the countryside, where there was no chance of being influenced or told what to do by others - to hear her own voice. If she had one.

The sound of the dog fox barking again punctured her thoughts. Was it the same one as earlier - a loner in the valley? The bark sounded more like a warning than a call for mates. She pictured him then, standing with his front legs apart and head bent low, facing someone or something on a path… just as there was a shuffling noise outside. She held her breath. What was that? A footstep? Sounded like branches being moved aside…

Suddenly there was a heavy thud on the other side of the bedroom wall and she sat bolt upright, clutching the blankets. Her heart was banging hard against her ribs. Whoever or whatever it was, they were so close as to be less than a foot away from her head.

She dared not even breathe.

The candlelight danced to the hypnotic drum of the rainfall. Her mind raced. This was the only cottage for possibly half a mile or more. Nearest house was the Moodys' farm. She was shivering from head to foot. Could it have been a deer? Or maybe it hadn't happened at all? As the minutes passed she convinced herself of that. Yes, one or the other – a deer or some other wild animal; or her own imagination. Slowly, soundlessly, she reached for her phone, and was staring at what was an unresponsive screen, realising there was no connection, when there was another solid thump.

Wide eyed, she willed herself to stay calm. The door was locked. Yes, definitely. And the only window other than in the kitchen was this one.

Lauren closed her eyes and prayed for protection. All she'd wanted was a little time off from the drama, an opportunity to reassess her life. But what if she'd made a terrible mistake coming here? Not another soul knew where she was.

***

CHAPTER TWO

After sitting up on high alert for a good half hour, Lauren finally acknowledged there was zero chance of sleep. An icy cloud had floated through the skin of her back and her toes were numb. She could feel the wire of the bedsprings beneath the mattress, and still the rain pelted down. It bounced off the tiles and spattered against the windows. And from somewhere inside the cottage a steady drip had started. Closing her eyes, she squeezed away the threatened tears. Maybe it was the fear, or the cold, or because events were catching up with her, but all at once loneliness hit hard. Why was she so absolutely alone? Thirty-two, an honest woman with a loving heart, yet there was no one. Not a single true friend. No family. No one on earth she could even phone to ask for help.

Maybe that was why Sebastian had found it so easy to play her for a fool? It had taken five years to see the light. By which time career, friends, savings and self-respect had been eradicated. How the hell had he done it?

And why did I let him?

Her breath plumed on the air as she pushed back the blankets, grabbed a dressing gown and hugged herself to keep warm. The only form of heating was a small electric fire in the kitchen, but even a chair next to that was preferable to lying in bed waiting for pneumonia to set in.

A flash of blue sparked at the electric socket as she switched on the kettle but thankfully the bars of the fire cranked into life. Meanwhile the rainstorm was upping a gear, pummelling the roof like a car wash.

Glancing upwards Lauren grimaced. "Please God, let it hold!"

Ooh, what was that? Déjà-vu? A fragment of having been as cold as this before, a long time ago, hovered on the edge of her mind again, then fluttered away. There had been a childhood holiday somewhere - a long track and green fields either side...No, it had gone...That was odd, though. As far as she could remember, Auntie Claire had only taken her on holiday once, and that had been a summer one to the beach.

The kettle boiled and she made tea, relishing the heat in her fingers as she clasped the cup. The advertisement for Clingbine Cottage had appeared in the local paper at half the rental price of everything else on the page - a whole cottage for less than a room-share in the dingiest most crime-ridden part of town. She'd found herself staring at the ad. Described as remote, ideal as a writing retreat or for a keen walker, it was in the middle of the Welsh Marches on the border between England and Wales.

At the time, traffic was roaring past the flat she'd rented above a café on the high street, and someone was stomping up and down on the floorboards above. In boots by the sound of it! She couldn't hear herself think. Every small irritation was one too many. And more urgently - the rental would run out at the end of the following week, she was struggling to pay, hadn't yet found another job and was finding it hard to face each day.

Desperate was never a good place to be...

Still staring at the ad, she'd put a star next to it. Nothing was working out for her here, all doors closing. What were the answers? God, she was so, so tired. Maybe just some time out?

Now, staring into the bars of the electric fire, she took a sip of camomile tea. It scorched her throat, the heat hit her stomach, and gratefully she drank more. Clarity of mind was the reason she was here and every day must count. There could be no more catastrophic mistakes. No more decisions based on what someone else wanted. It never worked, she realised that now - if you didn't do what was right for yourself then eventually you'd be forced to address it one way or the other, and none of those you'd listened to would be around to pick up the pieces. Besides, there was very little money left, so the next decision had to be a good one!

Panic rose at her predicament and she tamped it down. It would be okay. It would. Tomorrow the heating would be fixed and after that she'd go into town. And it had probably just been a deer outside. She'd got herself into a state. The place was beautiful and this would be good… it was steeped in history and there was no doubting its mysterious beauty. The entire area for miles around was densely forested, spread over hills and dales with the Welsh mountains of Snowdonia in the distance. And with more castles per square mile than anywhere else on earth, there was an almost fairy tale quality to it.

She took another sip, gradually thawing, soothing herself with tea and warmth and logic. According to an online description, the estate belonged to D'Avranches Grange, an ancient family seat that could be traced back hundreds of years. And Groom Lake appeared to be one of the few villages left in Britain that was still entirely owned by the ruling family. This seemed to consist of the Moodys' farm and a few derelict buildings passed on the way here. Buildings or building? She frowned, unable to remember because on arrival she'd been searching for the gates to the estate and hadn't properly taken stock. Going by the name though, there ought to be a lake. She hadn't noticed one. That was odd. So where was the rest of the village?

"I wonder why they rented out this cottage?" she asked out loud. "And why now?"

It was so dilapidated, so…desolate…

Back came the sense of unease. It clutched at her stomach and gnawed into her mind. And as the doubts crept in once more, shadows broke away from the walls and began to move around. They were caused by the candle in the bedroom, she told herself, the glow of the fire, and the draught from under the door.

And she kept on telling herself this even when the candle faltered and night plunged into the darkest hour. No human being had occupied these deathly damp rooms for decades, whispered her inner voice. No one living...

All will be well…it will be okay…

Daylight soon!

***

CHAPTER THREE

By three in the morning, however, the fatigue was so overpowering she could no longer stay awake. Nor could she remember putting down the cup or closing her eyes, but it was around that time – when half asleep, half awake – that the cottage walls began to merge with the surrounding woods, and an unfamiliar tug inside pulled her down into the deep undercurrent of a disturbingly lucid dream. Was she awake or asleep? What was real and what was not?

Unlike the lush forests covering the surrounding hills, the woods behind the cottage had a touch of death about them, the interior a gloomy cathedral of regimental pines planted in lieu of the original trees. A crescent moon flitted in between a canopy of needles; and a low whine blew off the mountains.

She had a feeling Clingbine Cottage was nearby, and that it would be there should she turn around. In dreamy slow motion she looked over her shoulder, and there it was - a cottage with a dull glow behind kitchen curtains that didn't quite meet in the middle. That was it. Definitely. And there was her car, a black Mini, parked to one side by the five bar gate. Was she out of body?

Yet there was no urge to go back. Instead she turned to face the woods again, and began to venture in, silent as a wraith. No sound came from within - not a single owl hoot, shriek or ke-wick, ke-wick; no fox barks or rustling in the undergrowth from nocturnal creatures - just the soughing of the wind and rainwater methodically dripping into mud. It occurred to her that she must be sleeping inside the cottage yet here she was outside. Was her body slumped on the chair by the fire? How strange, she thought, continuing the journey - as strange as a dream could be, while being conscious of every nuance.

Her eyes were starting to adjust, noticing now that shapes were shifting and separating from tree trunks and undergrowth, to form a crowd of grey figures. It looked as if a grave had been raised, and its newly surfaced inhabitants were inquisitive and astonished enough to step out from the shadows. A thousand eyes peered out of the gloom as she felt herself pulled ever deeper into the core of the forest. The trees seemed not to breathe, the hushed interior cold as a stone cellar, unstirred by the tunnel of echoing wind in the canopy.

The sensation crept over her then as it had on the hill – a feeling someone was on the path behind - and a clutch of unease tightened inside.

I want to wake up!

Right on cue a man's laugh broke out directly next to one ear, just as if he walked alongside, and she winged around.

The path was empty. Not a soul was there. For a while she stood and stared, her heart thumping hard, fast and loud. An air of quiet menace had descended so surreptitiously as to have occurred without notice. Now it crawled up her spine, and a foul and fetid stench permeated the air. Had that happened suddenly, too, or had she only just become aware of it? Was it stagnant water? Compost? Something rotting?

The cottage light was a mere orb in the distance now and there was no going back: the invisible presence on the path was between her and the body which lay sleeping inside it.

Later, much later, when she recalled the strange lucid dream, she acknowledged it had felt fateful, as if she must continue the journey; and once more, as if hypnotised, she turned to face the path, gravitating towards something that pulled her as strongly as a magnet. It seemed she drew the curious along, too - the grey spectres floating towards her, joining her on a path that was spiralling anti-clockwise, coiling into a central point like water swirling into a drain. A bad drain, she thought. The stale odour was fortifying. She tried to place it...sulphur...sewage...rotten eggs...but laced with some other indefinable thing. There was a feeling of lack here, of there being nothing, of abandonment, and desolation. Even the wind did not breathe life into the empty, hollow shell of these woods.

She kept walking, almost gliding, entranced, when a raucous scream rent the silence and she paused, confused. The echo rang through the woods. An owl?

Yes, a screech owl. Must have been.

And just as she'd decided that was the case, and had resumed the trance-like pull towards the centre of the woods, the sound of running feet pounded rapidly behind, forcing her to leap out of the way as whoever it was bolted past - a quick panting breath – then vanished, instantly enveloped by the blackness.

Wake up, Lauren!

But she could not wake, even when the dream then

plunged rapidly and unmistakeably into the abyss of a nightmare. The whole place suddenly seethed, having become a thick, palpable mass of whispering, visible entities. Her heart lurched. Everything had changed, from dreamily strange to alarming. The ghostly figures were not benign. And they were drawing closer, too close – claw hands reaching out as more and more rose from the undergrowth. The effect was one of unnatural coldness, a grey mist winding its way to the heart of the woods, dragging her along in a current impossible to resist.

The path had become noticeably narrower too, with high hedges bordering either side. Where was this leading? The centre was now so close. Oh God, what would there be to face? Something terrible? The stench of bad drains was overwhelming, yet she could not stop the momentum and the sheer power of the magnetic force pulling them all towards it.

Glancing over her shoulder, she half expected to see someone running up behind her as she flowed with the now unstoppable tide. When unexpectedly there was a vaguely familiar noise. She tried to make sense of it: a horn blown, and shouts…

Was it a hunting party? There! It came again. Yes, a hunting horn! A hunt! A clatter of hooves thundering along one of the paths. She cast around this way and that. Which path? From which direction were they coming?

When suddenly a group of riders was upon her.

Their voices were as babbled as a fast flowing brook and all she caught was a blur of moonlit faces smeared with red, and then a tangle of spurs, bleeding flanks and yanked reins, before they turned en-masse and raced back through the trees, vanishing as quickly as they'd appeared into a night punctuated with screams.

Who was screaming? She tried to discern. There were commanding excited shouts, but also the quick light sound of bare feet pummelling the path, the pulse of rapid heartbeats, and the short sharp gasps of those whose breath was about to give out. Faces loomed in and out of the darkness - scratched, bleeding flesh and wild eyes. They were running flat out, she realised. Running for their lives! Hearts about to burst!

Her own heart was banging so hard in her chest she could barely breathe. This was just a dream. Not real. A nightmare.

Wake up! Wake up!

The curiosity, however, was too strong. And ignoring the voice of warning, the call to come back to the surface world, she moved instead with the flow, allowing herself to be carried along on its sickly swell.

Must see…must see…

Until finally there it was: a pool of stagnant water. A lake.

But someone was there!

The second she realised someone was standing on the path, blocking the way, the lake became a background haze, the bizarre sweep of the ghostly race abruptly over. Everything fell away, the night cleared to starlit, and it was just the two of them.

Lauren stared at the small figure as if her whole life had led to this. Recognition jolted through her while simultaneously having no idea who she was.

A young girl was squinting into the darkness as if she couldn't quite believe her eyes. A girl dressed in a blue mac and wellington boots with flowers on them.

About seven or eight years old, she was standing in the woods at night on her own in the rain. Behind her the lake glistened darkly, and as each stared at the other dumbfounded, moonlight swept over the grounds and Lauren caught a brief impression of D'Avranches Grange. Long and low, the building was nestled into the base of the hill, almost concealed by the trees, with the ruins of Woodsay Castle flitting in and out of scudding clouds high above.

The girl was looking directly at Lauren with an unflinching piercing stare and had begun to walk towards her with firm purpose.

Lauren's heart rate picked up.

But am I not in a dream? What can she see? Surely nothing...

Events happened then, too fast to comprehend. At the very moment Lauren realised the girl really could see her and was speaking, another figure stepped behind the child. At which point, very softly at first, a low hum began, amplifying by degrees from every corner of the woods.

It filled her head in seconds. Goose bumps shivered up and down her back, and then the dream flipped as surely as if she'd stared too long into a mirror and fallen through the back of it. The gloomy light switched to total blackness, the hum rose to an insufferable high-pitched whistle, and a voice yelled inside her head, "Get out, Lauren! Now!"

The trance broke in an instant and she fled back through the trees. But the cottage light seemed too dim, too far away, and no matter how fast she ran the distance wasn't closing. The knowledge hit her with a sickly thud as still in dream state she tried frantically to understand what was happening: her legs were on a treadmill to nowhere, running but not gaining ground, stationary. And a great mass of blackness, all the dark entities that had swept her towards the lake, was surging up behind. Another second and it would envelop her completely into whatever endless horror they perpetuated and endured. The weight was leaden, the energy too powerful.

It's not real...not real...

Desperately she willed herself out of what had rapidly become the trap of a nightmare.

I'm stuck...I can't get out!

***

CHAPTER FOUR

When Lauren was finally shocked out of the dream it was with a sudden and violent white flash. Her heart was hammering, skin covered in a sheen of cold sweat.

It took a while to accept her surroundings again, for the dismal kitchen to recreate itself - the bright orange bars of the heater, the stainless steel sink and swan's neck tap, the gap in the curtains… Her breath steamed on the night air, the room quiet as a grave apart from the sound of branches scratching against a window at the back. Or was it someone tapping? She tuned back in, instantly recalling the intruder earlier. How could she have fallen asleep? The bad dream was over – that's all it was! But this was real. Was someone still there? The moment stretched out.

A blind in the bathroom rattled of its own accord.

How could that be with no window open? And no draught?

Then it stopped.

No, there was nothing. It had just been her imagination - she was out here alone, had been spooked by a wild animal outside and then had a nightmare. That was all, she told herself. All explainable. Although the dream had been very lucid. And out of body. Frowning, she picked up her phone. Still no signal. Not even one bar. Dear God, this was like something out of a horror movie. All it took was slashed tyres and... A projection of herself running frantically through the woods shot into her mind - branches ripping at her face as the pursuer closed the gap between them, a laugh ricocheting around the forest...

Lauren, for God's sake get a grip!

She huddled over the cranking bars of the heater. She was going to frighten herself to death here. You could actually make things happen, she'd read once – thoughts could manifest, and the more you worried the more worry would come your way, such was the law of physics, of the universe. It was important to think of good things, expand the positive. All would be well, it would!

Yet here that seemed impossible. The cold was the icy damp of a cave, the air heavy and oppressive. A shiver spread across her back. 'Stop being so scared', she scolded herself. The door was locked. No one could get in. And who the hell would be out here at this time of night, anyway? Gradually she calmed her breathing, focusing on the here and now, persuading herself that out of body experiences were common, that it was nothing more than that, just a first for herself. She would be sure to read up on it more, and then be less afraid of the unknown.

The old ash trees lining the lane by the gates rustled and shook. Daylight was coming...soon... soon... She leant back and closed her eyes, training her mind to think only of practical things and not to relive and thus embed the nightmare, which far from fading remained imprinted in all its lurid detail. It wanted to replay, to flash the girl's face before her mind's eye, nagging and insistent.

She pushed it away, forcing in new thoughts. Tomorrow the boiler would be fixed, and it would make sense to go and buy more provisions - maybe pop into

Owlbury town centre for a portable heater and some decent blankets? Also, she'd go up to the Moodys' farm and make sure they were going to do it. Glynis had been far too flippant. This was supposed to be a bloody holiday cottage! Comfortable!

Three o'clock in the morning slipped seamlessly into four o'clock, and briefly, just at the moment where coherent thoughts blended with those of dreams, she was jolted awake again. No, she mustn't drop off. What if the nightmare resumed?

But the strange magnetic pull was a powerful one and she felt herself transported as surely as crossing a road, from one side to the other. Her own voice murmured and she heard the words of warning as if they came from someone else, but could not resist. And the next time she was conscious it was once again to find herself outside of her own body. Later she would remember every last detail of this one, too – as clearly as a memory and not any kind of dream at all.

She was standing alone, a silent watcher on the top of Nine Rings Hill. The wind was whining through the castle ruins, and the line of men in long hooded cloaks was gliding past just as they had a matter of hours before. Her hair was whipping back from her face, the scene playing out in slow motion. One of the figures seemed to sense her presence, stiffening slightly, but did not look back.

Who are you?

Then, again as before, each in turn vanished off the side of the cliff into thin air. It was like standing on the top of the world - forests and mountains stretching out below as far as the eye could see - hundreds and hundreds of acres of trees, valleys and hills in the dark velvet tapestry of night.

The place was beautiful, magnificent, yet whatever lay beneath the hill felt static and decidedly off-kilter.

In sleep she muttered and stirred, drifting now into a gilt-edged wooded valley bathed in the haze of autumnal gold. The colours were surreal, the atmosphere intense. Coppery leaves danced beneath a deep azure sky, the forest glades alive with deer, rabbits and pheasants. Wending its way through the valley a river sparkled with water as clear as crystal, and boughs of trees sang with hidden birds. She honed in on a three storey building positioned on the corner of a track - a stone mill with a large wheel to one side, beyond it a gateway just before a ford. It seemed vaguely familiar and she looked over to a field where a circle of people in white had gathered by the river.

This is here…the mill and the ford…the ring of people in white… it's here…

But as soon as the recognition began to click into place, she rapidly surfaced from the dream and lurched awake. A single grey shaft of light now filtered through the curtains above the kitchen sink. Never had she been so thankful to see the light of dawn. Thank God the night was over. Those dreams were nothing like any dream she'd ever had before, and were so real they were going to linger, she was sure.

After a cup of tea followed by a lightning fast strip-wash in cold water, Lauren tied her hair up, dressed, then set off for the Moodys' farm. As part of this agreement the cottage should be heated, and they could have had the decency to check that out. There was no way she could possibly spend another night like that. Probably she'd had such bizarre dreams due to the onset of a fever? Delirium? Pneumonia even?

Spurred into action and tetchy from lack of sleep, she decided to walk the half mile or so, largely because the steep track up to the Moodys' farm was pitted with potholes and had nearly taken the suspension out of her old Mini the day before. It wasn't far, and besides, the fresh air would be invigorating.

Their farm was an L-shaped brick bungalow that stood to one side of a wind-blasted field at the top of the hill, just before it became woodland. Tyler Moody's Landrover was parked in front of the lounge window, and a dog that began to bark as she approached, had been chained to a kennel. A tumble of straw blew across a yard at the back; and as her gaze flicked back to the house a blind twitched.

Panting after the climb, Lauren paused for a moment to recover her breath. She hadn't really noticed yesterday, but it looked as though this had once been a thriving farm. Now, however, all that remained were the foundations of an old piggery and several dilapidated barns. She looked around. No sheep… No animals of any sort… No crops…

As she approached, the front door was flung wide and a slightly built, dark-haired man watched her walk the rest of the way up the path.

"Hi!" she called out, still short of breath.

Unshaven, with deep lines etching his eyes and mouth, there seemed something about him that was strangely lacking without a shotgun in his hand.

"I'm Lauren, from your holiday cottage?"

He stared at her for a long uncomfortable minute, then turned to the dog and snapped, "Shut it!"

"Thought I'd walk up but it's quite a trek. Not as fit as I thought."

"Who is it?" Glynis called.

"It'll be the missus you need," he said, grabbing a waxed jacket from a hook by the door. "You can wait inside."

This was not a home, Lauren thought as she thanked him and stepped into the porch. This was a holding bay. The stink of fried bacon greased the kitchen walls and coated the paintwork, a bluish haze still tinging the air.

Outside, the dog's barks lessened to intermittent, Tyler's Landrover sprayed gravel as it accelerated away, and the house settled, the only sound now that of a television droning from upstairs. Glimpsed through an archway the lounge was a clash of orange and brown, bare apart from a large television set dominating most of one wall, a PVC sofa, and a coffee table strewn with mugs and an overloaded ash tray.

"Can I help you?"

She jumped. "Ooh, sorry. Yes, your husband said I should wait here for you. I came about the boiler because–"

"Bit early, isn't it?" said Glynis Moody. "Haven't had breakfast yet." Her face was puffy, hair iron-flat at the back. "Want a cup of tea, do you?"

The smell of the kitchen wafted over.

"No thanks, you're okay. It's just that the boiler really must be fixed. I was freezing last night. I can't even have a wash let alone a bath."

"I told you we'd sort it."

"Thank you, I know. But I wanted to ask when - if it would definitely be today?"

"Yes, today. He's had to go out but he'll be back later. I'll get him to come down this afternoon."

"All right, thank you. I've got to go into Owlbury again but I should be back by lunchtime. I'll wait in because I can't have another night as cold as that, it was–"

Glynis walked into the kitchen, scooped a packet of cigarettes off the table and shook one out. "Right you are."

"Well, I'll see you later then, your husband anyway–"

"Tyler. Expect him after two. After lunch, all right?"

"Oh, I know what I meant to ask – who owns the big house by the lake? I assume it's D'Avranches Grange?"

"Lord Landgrave." She flicked open a lighter. "Him and his wife. Court judge, isn't it?"

"Oh, I see. And have they always lived there? Is it, you know, a family seat or something? I should have researched it more, I suppose."

Glynis took a drag of her cigarette, taking her time to blow out the smoke. "Always, as far as I know, anyhow."

Without thinking she blurted out, "They must have children, then? I mean, I think I saw a little girl–" Then stopped, confused. Oh no, that had been a dream…the child in the flowery wellington boots… An age-old sensation of heat burned into her skin, the annoying fire of a blush rising in her cheeks.

Eyeing her calmly, Glynis shook her head. "No, I expect that's why they do what they do - because they don't have them."

"What do you mean?"

"Take troubled kids in, the ones you can't do anything with. Something to do with his charity, I think. Had an award for it, he has. From the Queen." Glynis reached for the kettle. "Anyhow, I must press on."

Lauren turned to go. "Oh yes, of course. Sorry. Thanks anyway."

The glass-panelled front door did nothing to stop the chill breezing into the porch, she thought, noting the curtain bunched to one side. The original farmhouse this had replaced would no doubt have had inglenook fireplaces and thick walls, but there was little in the way of creature comforts in this contraption. Letting herself out she hurried down the steps intending to leave straight away, but the dog, a collie, whined a little, and on instinct she walked over. He'd probably been trained to bark his head off at intruders but there was something about him that seemed to yearn for attention.

Stopping slightly short of arm's reach, she dropped to her haunches. "What's your name, then?"

Head down, he regarded her steadily.

"It's okay. I just wanted to say, 'Hello.'"

A shiny well-gnawed bone lay on the floor nearby and her heart went out to him. How dependent animals were on humans. Was Tyler Moody kind to him? Was Tyler a good man with a moral compass? *Or not?*

Despite having her back to the bungalow, she sensed Glynis staring through the blinds, smoking as she waited for the kettle to boil. Weighing her up? Wondering if she was going to ask for her money back?

A fresh breeze swept over the fields, and she looked over her shoulder at the distant rise of the Welsh mountains silhouetted against a bullet-grey sky. There was something else she'd meant to ask Glynis, but what was it? Dizzy with fatigue she swayed slightly, her thoughts suddenly drowned out by a rush of running water - water that came from almost every direction. It streamed down the fields and lanes in rivulets, rhythmically hypnotic, as she stared at the pot-holed drive leading down to the road, trying to recall what it was.

Better set back.

Her gaze then fell upon a stile leading into the woods. Oh yes, that was it - to ask if she could use the footpath through the Estate. It could save as much as twenty minutes between here and the cottage. About to go and knock on the door again, however, she hesitated. Actually, it could wait. She'd ask Tyler this afternoon.

The collie was now lying down with his head resting on his paws, still eyeing her. His kennel was dry and he didn't look badly treated. She reached out to him and his nose touched her hand, damp and cool.

"It will all be okay. You look okay. I think you get fed and watered, but maybe could do with a hug?" She stroked the side of his face and he leaned against her hand.

"Lots of love my friend, but I'd better go."

As she stood to leave, it occurred to her that if she was to cut back through the woods over the stile, no one would know. What harm would it do? Besides, part of her wanted to find out if there was any truth in the dream, and if the lake was where the dream had taken her. For a second she thought about it. Then again, what if Glynis was watching? No, maybe she'd explore from the direction of the cottage. Yes, that would probably be best.

It was beginning to spit rain, so Lauren put her head down against the wind and hurried down the drive deep in thought. Rescue children, Glynis had said. Maybe the girl was one of those? But if she was real and not just part of a ghostly dream, then what was she doing wandering around on her own at the dead of night in pouring rain? The thing was, the child's face and expression was still as clear in her mind as if she'd known her all her life.

Glynis's stare was burning a hole in Lauren's back and it took an iron will not to turn around as she tramped down the drive.

And someone was snooping around outside the cottage last night! I know they were. It wasn't a deer. A deer wouldn't crash into the side of a house.

So was there anyone else living here in the village? Another night lay ahead. There'd been a few buildings further up the road. But what about a mill? Was there a mill on a bend with a wheel to one side? Had she passed one? What if it looked exactly as it had in the dream? She nodded to herself. Would the lake and the house also look as they had in the dream? She felt something dislodge in her mind then, an intangible fragment that floated away just out of reach.

And by the time she got to the bottom of the drive she'd made a decision: well, it wouldn't hurt to find out.

***

CHAPTER FIVE

Groom Lake was such a tiny hamlet it didn't even merit a name plate. The only way Lauren had found it yesterday was by following the directions Glynis had sent over: 'Don't use satnav or you'll end up in a field. Come off the A49 south at the Dancing Green Pub, go for two miles until you see the sign for Ladies' Gate, then take a left and continue a good mile, then left again at the cattle grid by the old telephone box at Bridle Corner. Follow this until you see a sign on the right for Groom Lake. It's a single track but keep going to where it dips sharply just before a ford. You'll see the gates to D'Avranches Grange on the left, and the cottage is just there.'

After leaving the Moodys' farm, Lauren retraced her steps along the lane. Certainly there were no other houses on the road between here and Owlbury. But what about in the other direction – the way she'd driven in? It might be useful to know, especially if someone was prowling around. Her imagination began to work on overdrive as once again she questioned the wisdom of an isolated retreat.

Walking past the cottage Lauren continued up the lane. The sound of rushing water was even more intense in the valley. Fresh and cold, it gushed from the hills, hidden streams gurgled in the forest, and the jutting rocks and dry stone walls were covered in moss.

She'd definitely passed a building yesterday. But where?

After about quarter of a mile there was a bend on the track, and the startling sight of a three storey stone house on the corner came into view. Stunned, she hurried towards it.

I've seen it before!

With a curved wall flush to the lane, the mill's windows were small and high. She crossed over for a closer look. And then her heart did a little flip. There, to one side, was a huge, albeit rusty and clearly disused, water wheel. A feeling then of timelessness and disorientating déjà-vu swept over her, and she held onto the dry stone wall, scrutinising the windows for signs of life. Did anyone live here? The frames were rotten though, and a few glass panes were broken. It looked derelict, as if it hadn't been occupied for years. So much for being able to call on neighbours if needed!

She walked as far as the corner, to where a single forest track veered off the lane, and here at the side of the mill, adjacent to a yard and various ramshackle outbuildings, was a wrought iron gate. She put her hand on the latch and then hesitated. It was an unnerving sensation, almost as if someone was waiting for her. Yet the place was without doubt abandoned…Weeds had grown between the cracks in the paving slabs, and winds of neglect whined through the broken window panes. Ivy had prised mortar from the stone walls, wired itself into the eaves and covered the roof tiles. It had even spread across the ground, spiralled into fruitless trees and smothered what had once been flower beds.

Someone's watching!

Instinctively she glanced up.

It was as if the spirits of the house were eyeing her from

an unlit shell, a fleeting glimpse of pale faces peering down… And then a movement. Very slight. Someone who instantly stepped back into the shadows.

Oh my God, it's lived in!

Her glance flicked to a bell on a rope by the front door. She pictured standing on the porch as the sound rang through those cavernous rooms, the reclusive inhabitant standing as motionless and silent as a sentinel.

He would not answer. Did not want to be seen. Was he the one who'd been snooping around the cottage last night? What to do? Should she, having been spotted, go ahead and ring the bell anyway?

Behind the yard, a steep bank of woods rose up to the moors. The noise of the brook racing down to the deep mill pond that swilled around the water wheel, filled the air with dizzying chatter. The effect was overpoweringly hypnotic and the sing-song chorus of an old nursery rhyme carried on the air… '*Ring-a-Ring o' roses… A pocket full of posies… A-tishoo! A-tishoo! We all fall down…*'

There was the oddest sensation of being caught in time, of being swept back many hundreds of years. Her hand dropped from the latch on the gate and she stepped away. Perhaps it had been the combination of tiredness and lingering dreams, but the moment had passed and she shook her head, deciding to walk a little further on to see if there were any more houses. The lane, however, continued winding around more and more bends, until finally it began to ascend out of the valley and the terrain changed to open fields. She turned around. Okay, well that was the answer then! Just one house. Which made the shadowy man at the dilapidated mill the only near neighbour.

She headed back, hands deep in pockets as the rain spat

in gusts. God, the place was so damp! What would it be like in January if it was as cold and wet as this in October?

The plan was to go into Owlbury before Tyler hopefully came to fix the boiler. But her thoughts would not turn to practicalities. Instead, fragments of last night's lucid dreams toyed with her mind as she hurried along, acutely aware of just how alone she was, of her footsteps echoing dully on the waterlogged lane, and the chill hush of the forest.

Memories surged in – of the mass of dark spectres floating to the lake, sharp screams piercing the night air, the overpowering sewer stench, and pounding footsteps so close there'd been a waft of air as whoever it was ran past. She'd heard their heartbeats, absorbed their fear, every detail easily recaptured. And the little girl! What age had she been? Seven? Eight? In her mind their eyes locked once more. The child had seen her, had looked surprised... Standing alone in the pouring rain at three in the morning...

Do what they do?

Take troubled kids in - the ones you can't do anything with. Something to do with his charity, I think.

Questions queued up in her mind as she drew level once more with the mill and slowed down to glance over at the windows.

There! Again a shadow passed behind the broken panes, but... She stopped and stared, open mouthed. Not just one. But a horde!

She stood riveted, unable to move despite knowing she was being watched. But were they alive or...in spirit?

Before coming to Groom Lake she'd never seen so much as a ghost, yet here the past intermingled with the living in a dance of shadows, time blurring at the edges – history an interwoven tapestry with the present. What was it about this place? It felt so…disconcerting…

The groan of a door swinging open at the back of the house, followed by the clink of bottles caused her to jump visibly. Footsteps clear and quick. A man was walking along the garden path towards the wrought iron gate and would see her.

Damn!

She made to move away. But it was too late. As he lifted the latch he stopped and pointedly turned to face her, a black rubbish bag clutched in one hand. Their eyes met. Blood pulsed loudly in her ears, the moment an adrenalin fuelled blur.

What had she expected? Possibly an older man, one living rough, a tramp? Definitely not one in his early thirties. As dark, lean and wily looking as Tyler Moody, he stared without so much as a blink. Dark eyes glinted beneath thick eyebrows that met in the middle, and he wore a long, black jacket and working boots. That's all she saw. She wanted to run but couldn't. To say something, anything, but couldn't. The moment locked and held until eventually he nodded. A curt nod. Before throwing the bag onto the grass verge and walking back inside.

They had refuse collections here? That's all she could think. Bin collections. So he wasn't a squatter?

The busy chatter of the brook and the rain pattering in the trees gave her the oddest feeling of floating as she hurried back to the cottage, perversely gratified to see the now familiar sight of the five bar gate. Her head was light and dizzy with vertigo as if nothing was quite real. She couldn't put her finger on what it was. But as she neared the entrance to D'Avranches Grange, a shaft of low sunlight illuminated the tops of the mountains with an aura of burnished gold, and all at once the hypnotic sound of racing water became dominant. She levelled with the gate just as leaves began to rise and swirl upwards from the forest floor, blowing into the road, flying around her head. The scenery blurred in an instant - gone the copper penny leaves dangling from branches, pine trees spiking into the clouds, and the outline of the gates. Shapes and colours had now combined to form a fluid collage that merged with her own body. All became one, swimming together in a giant watercolour, the effect both unnerving and magical.

Something's going to happen. Something coming!

A roar like an oncoming train…

There was no time, no time at all, and she almost fell against the low stone wall bordering the lane, such was the speed and power of the car that sped past. Nor did the driver slow down, having almost knocked someone to the ground, but instead shot through the entrance to D'Avranches Lodge and accelerated up the drive. Blacked-out windows, was the only detail she had the wherewithal to note.

She was brushing grit from her hands, shaking from head to foot and muttering, "Charming! I mean, bloody hell! Was that Lord Landgrave? Well, at least we know who did all the road kills…" When the car ground to a halt and began to reverse.

***

Chapter Six

He buzzed down the passenger-side window and peered out. Reflective sunglasses. White shirt. Dark hair swept back, curling into the nape of his neck. The dashboard had a black glass computer screen spanning its entire length, the interior plush red leather.

"Who are you?"

She reeled at the unexpected accusatory tone, temporarily lost for words.

"I, um…" The word, 'Sorry' was on the edge of her tongue but she bit it back. "You nearly knocked me over."

"And you are? Who?"

She fumbled for the stone gatepost behind and quickly rationalised she was on the man's property and probably obliged to answer. "I'm at the cottage," she said, wishing she didn't sound so defensive, so childlike, so small. The car was a great, shiny black tank of a thing with a neon-lit dash, and him high up in a colossal armchair. "Mrs Moody rented it out -from up at the farm."

He stared for an uncomfortably long time, and then, as a cloud passes over the sun, the moment brightened, and a wide slow smile spread across his face. "Has she really? I didn't know that."

Lauren nodded and was just about to ask who he was, when he buzzed the window up. "Take better care, anyway.

We don't want you run over now, do we?"

After the car had roared away, she stood looking at Clingbine Cottage, which squatted in its dismal corner. Built for a gatekeeper or a farmhand? And why would Lord Landgrave not use the considerably more grand entrance at the front? This was most definitely the farming end of the estate, with mud all churned up, narrow water-logged lanes, and stone walls coated in lichen. She shook her head. Then again, why not?

Inside the cottage she switched on the kettle and the electric fire. The air was far colder inside than out, as icy as a tomb. Was that because it hadn't been occupied in such a long time? It seemed, she thought, more than that, though. The student digs she'd once lived in hadn't had heating. The house had been a run-down Victorian terrace on a main road, the clothes in the old mahogany wardrobe musty, tide marks of damp on the bedroom walls. They'd all had a little fan heater and slept in woollens. But even that hadn't been as bone chilling as this place.

As the kettle bubbled to life and the bars of the fire cranked, she sat down and hugged herself to keep warm. If the boiler didn't get fixed this afternoon she couldn't stay. Problem was - would Glynis refund her? The prospect of asking the woman seemed formidable. Oh God, what a mess! She hadn't predicted this, had trusted the place would be a comfortable sanctuary for a while. Well, hopefully Tyler would turn up. Why was she repeatedly in awkward, unsettled, downright regrettable situations? These things didn't happen to anyone else she knew.

Poor you, Lauren! Oh how, awful for you! I suppose I'm lucky with my family ...

Tears smarted her eyes. Money was tight now and she

had no job, career, or support of any kind. In truth, she was utterly alone. The last big mistake had been to allow a man to take her apart piecemeal. She could see it now – the twist of contempt on his face one day, the laconic amusement the next. She was pretty useless, apparently. Her past was risible, her nursing job was 'pin money,' and her mental state obsessive and needy in turn. There had once been a family wedding on his side, and she'd driven a long way only to find she hadn't been seated. Sebastian had told her not to make a fuss, but to go and wait in the bar. She'd slept with him later, had eaten crisps and chocolate from the mini fridge in his room while everyone else drank champagne downstairs.

She put her head in her hands as the kettle came to the boil. How low she had sunk! He'd been right all along – without him she had nothing at all, had fallen off life's conveyor belt, and quite simply slipped off it unnoticed.

Oh, how awful for you…

Perhaps she lost consciousness for a moment, maybe due to extreme fatigue. Or had regret, fear and shame left her empty, lacking, and unguarded? Either way, the effect was as seamless as the night before. One minute she'd been thinking coherently and the next she was living another reality, every bit as intense as if it was taking place right now. She was falling into something soft - an eiderdown and pillows - tapestries hung on the walls, and through a leaded window pane there were treetops spearing a starry sky. Lying flat, she was unable or unwilling to move, the atmosphere one of almost unearthly stillness. But the emotional pain building up inside was no dream. It was ripping through her like a surgical knife cutting through flesh, erupting from the depths of her soul, overwhelming, all-consuming, and far too much to bear.

Catapulted out of the momentary trance, her hands flew to her face and she doubled over as raw, racking sobs broke freely. What was this pain? This terrible, terrible pain? The pain of what? Everything she would never have?

"Oh God, please help me, I'm lost. What's happening to me? I'm so, so lost..."

It was a long time before the grief subsided enough for her to notice the silence of the kettle and the frost of her breath on the air. Dabbing at her face, she glanced at the time. How much had passed? An hour? Had she been sitting here for an hour? Really?

Although it was still morning, there was a lot to do today and it was important not to risk missing Tyler Moody later: facing another freezing, sleepless night was not an option. Propelling herself into action, she quickly made tea and toast, then grabbed her bag and car keys and set off for Owlbury. What did she need? She thought back to her student days - a fan heater, blankets, food...So some kind of camping centre or country store! There was bound to be one.

It felt good to be back in the Mini driving out of the valley, more normal somehow. It was only when she reached open moorland, however, that she noticed how dramatic the change actually was – akin to surfacing from a deep-sea dive. Immediately the world seemed lighter. With the heater blasting onto her feet, she zapped down the window and took several grateful breaths of fresh air. Here, high above the clouds, the day was considerably brighter and breezier than the sopping chilly one below; and this time she made sure to note her surroundings. Were there any houses? What were the landmarks? On the right hand corner at the T-junction with the main road, there was a pub - an old travellers' inn that still had stables out back. On all sides, boggy moorland stretched out for mile upon mile, the black and white timbered building looking as if it had hunkered down against centuries of battering wind and rain. Closed to custom, Fiddlers Elbow now stood empty though, its jaunty roadside sign swinging gently on a rusty chain.

At the point of turning right for Owlbury, she noted the rough bridle track opposite, instantly picturing a Dickensian style stagecoach disappearing into the fog, swaying with lanterns and loaded luggage. Probably this had once been a crossroads. There was a raw sense of history here that lingered; layers that time had done nothing to erase.

And the feeling of time having bled through the years persisted, when fifteen minutes later she was walking along Owlbury's cobbled high street. 'Quaint' did not adequately describe it, she thought. This was to be transported back hundreds and hundreds of years. Medieval in appearance, three and four storey timber-framed buildings with tiny leaded windows, leaned towards each other over the road like gossips. Low-ceilinged with sloping floors, most of them were now shops and cafés with varnished wooden interiors and private courtyards at the back. The town was in possession of a kind of fairy tale beauty, an enchantment preserved almost intact. And where the streets all tipped down to meet in a convergence at the foot of the hill, a wide shallow river ran under a bridge. Swans sailed past on the current, shafts of sunlight catching on the ripples.

Surveying the picturesque scene, it crossed her mind, however, that something wasn't quite right about this small town. In the full five minutes she'd been standing there, not one car had crossed over the bridge - neither in, nor out. And the other side led to the outer world via a single ribbon of tarmac, which tapered into the distant hills. It was as if Owlbury, Lauren thought, functioned largely in isolation.

You always get things wrong, Lauren. You imagine things. You have a very skewed view of the world – you're not in reality...

Yes, she was probably mistaken. This was just an ordinary market town. On a perfectly average weekday.

But as she began to search for the kind of shop that might sell basic supplies, an uneasy feeling of being observed crept up on her, of being noted from within the dark oak interiors that creaked and whispered. It was too quiet. The town dozed. The buildings wavered in a haze of eerie light. And was the faint clip-clop of horses' hooves, the clatter of carts, and the chime of a shop doorbell also her imagination? Again, it was as if an invisible barrier had been crossed without noticing...and now, suddenly, history had come to life. Before her eyes, the main street had become a dirt track strewn with sawdust, the corn exchange boomed with the monotone of an auction, the market square was alive with flapping chickens, wagons full of grain...a man in breeches playing the flute on the town hall steps...The tune echoed down the ages, a lively ditty that carried on the brisk October air.

What on earth...? I'm going mad...must be...

By the time Lauren drew level with the church railings she felt faint and needed to sit down. The air was close and muggy, her limbs tired, mind foggy. The whole town crackled with white noise - a television station not tuned in.

She fancied she could see shadows skittering along building walls, that an ancient world was but a megahertz away, and all that was necessary to step into it would be consent…or maybe one drink too many…

The weight of the atmosphere dragged and pulled, and despite the clear sky day, the light had dimmed a little and the streets darkened as if a storm was coming. She wrapped her hands around the wrought iron railings and peered through, grateful for the coolness of the graveyard wafting onto her face; for the sense of peace. Long grass swayed amongst weather beaten headstones, and as she looked up at the spire it was to be struck anew by a sense of timelessness. At the far end, in a grove shaded by yews, was a well, conjuring memories of all the well dressings Auntie Claire had taken her to see. The significance of water - what was it, she thought, and why had she never asked? So many churches had been built over or near springs and wells. Why?

Having recovered a little, putting the disconcerting episode down to lack of sleep, she resumed the search, and in the end found the store she needed at the very top of a steep alley. It was the kind of shop that sold a little bit of everything, from pet food and spanners to barbecue sauce, paint and bedding. Lauren picked up a hot water bottle, fan heater, and a fleece-lined sleeping bag, adding a pillow and two army blankets before heading to the checkout.

"Phew! Think that's the lot."

The items were scanned with a price gun and dumped in a heap. "Sixty eight pounds, fifteen pence," said the cashier, a plump woman of indeterminable age.

"Would you have any carrier bags, please?"

Current eyes glared from out of a dough face weighted

with many chins. "One pound fifty for those."

"Think I'll need two, actually," Lauren said. The woman chucked them onto the pile. Jeez, what was wrong with her? She began to pack. "Thank you."

"Sorry," the woman said, turning to the couple behind as Lauren struggled to pack and pay at the same time. "Won't keep you long."

Seriously though, she thought, exiting the shop with currant-bun eyes boring into her back, what the fuck was that about? Could the woman not have helped? Whatever happened to manners? Why did the people behind her matter while she apparently did not? She found she was shaking with indignation. The world was full of bullies and never more so than here -every person who passed by seemed to bear a grudge, glancing up to glower as they levelled. What was wrong with them? Or her? Was it herself? As she hurried over to the deli, the town hall clock struck one o'clock, and propelled to urgency by Tyler's due visit, she stopped only to buy bread, cheese and jam before heading back to the car park.

"I'm going to run out of funds too quickly at this rate," she muttered to herself, piling up the car boot. She shouldn't have had to buy any of this stuff, hadn't factored this in at all. Rushing and already starting to worry about another night in the cottage, Lauren bent to pick up the rest of the shopping from the floor, then stood up too abruptly and banged her head. "Ow! Bloody hell, that's all I needed! For f..."

"Are you okay?"

She held onto the rim of the boot and tried to smile through the pain.

A woman was walking over.

"Sorry, um…yes."

"That was quite a bump. Are you sure?"

The most striking aspect of the stranger's appearance was without doubt the coil of shining silver hair on top of her head, quickly followed by her eyes, steady and grey. Tall, in a long skirt, boots, and a somewhat tatty sheepskin jacket, she stood out from a town of surly folk in jeans and anoraks.

"Yes, thanks," Lauren said, unable to help noticing the black obsidian, or was it tourmaline, adorning the woman's throat, wrists and fingers. She rubbed the top of her head, the crack of metal on bone still resounding through her skull. "Stupid. I was in a rush. I've got to get back to get the heating fixed."

"You've got heating? You're lucky."

She squinted at her through a haze of confusion. Déjà-vu. There it was again. So brief, so tantalising, as fleeting a visitor as an instantly forgotten dream. "Well, not exactly. I arrived last night to find it wasn't working. I was freezing. Honestly, I can't have another night like that one."

"I rented a place a month ago but there's no heating to fix. It's only got an open fire and an immersion heater for hot water."

"Oh, blimey!"

"Hopefully won't be here much longer, though. Anyway, as long as you're all right?" She was rooting for her car key, and had already turned towards a jeep parked alongside Lauren's Mini.

There was a certain down to earth quality about the accent. Lauren frowned.

I know her! Where from?

Her memory began to search its history vault, and then

a sense of urgency suddenly gripped her as the other woman unlocked her car door. "Erm..."

Oh God, what can I say?

The woman looked over her shoulder.

Lauren flushed. "Sorry again, but I just think I might know you from somewhere."

"Do you know I thought that, too?"

"Did you?"

"I was trying to think. It's Lauren, isn't it?"

"Lauren Stafford, yes." This was incredible. What were the odds? "So where–?"

"Oh, my goodness! I'm Hannah - Hannah Hardy. Yes, of course I remember you now. We worked on the wards together in Leeds!" She patted the silver nest on top of her head. "My hair used to be jet black back then."

Behind Hannah's head, sunlight splayed a hand of ethereal fingers across the mountains, and as she talked, their many months of chatting while changing bedsheets on the long nightingale wards, now replayed. Hannah had been different from the others – more independent - not lodging in the allocated student digs but in a rented studio of her own. She used to bring packed lunches instead of eating in the canteen, and had preferred to walk in the hospital grounds or read. Nor did she meet up in the pub after work. Didn't drink, Lauren remembered. The others hadn't liked that, had taken to bitching.

"You're miles from home," Lauren blurted out. Didn't Hannah originally come from Cumbria?

Hannah smiled, waves of sadness and regret instantly dampening her mood. "Ah, well...separation, a missing...I mean a kind of... Anyway, I've still got a place in the Lakes. I'm a healer."

A myriad of emotions was passing behind Hannah's eyes as she stumbled over her words, and Lauren jumped in to help ease the moment.

"Nursing?"

"No, spiritual healing. Animals, horses, and the earth - trees, lanes, even buildings, particularly bridges."

Lauren nodded. Bridges? You could heal bridges? "I've head of horse whisperers. Do you mean like that?"

"Yes, sort of. It's all energies, really. Everything is living and has an energy - a vibration, a frequency, and a consciousness. Even rocks!" She touched the dark crystal at her throat. "Oh!" Hannah reached into her pocket. "Here's my card if you want it. Mobile number's on the back. Where are you staying, by the way? Are you working here or–?"

"I'm on the D'Avranches Estate at Groom Lake - a cottage at the back of–" Lauren stopped talking. "What? What is it?"

Hannah's eyes had widened and kept on widening. Her eyebrows had almost reached her hairline before she spoke again.

"Are you serious? You're actually living at Groom Lake?"

"Um–"

"How long did you say you've been there, Lauren?"

"Just since last night." She picked up the bag with the heater in it. "Why?"

***

Chapter Seven

The whole conversation had left her floored, the impact impossible to shake off.

Lauren was accelerating out of town. Of all the people to bump into! And in such a remote place, too. It wasn't that so much though, as Hannah's face when she'd told her she was living at Groom Lake. Hannah had looked… What was the word? Horrified? Shocked? Sick? Her words echoed inside her head, 'I once went walking there but I had to turn back…'

She was so preoccupied it was a surprise to see Fiddlers Elbow, and she almost missed the turn. Once again the old inn looked deserted, the car park empty. She gave it but a cursory glance as she rounded the corner, however, before putting her foot down again. It was really important not to miss Tyler Moody. A track off to the right led to Groom Lake and she took the turn at speed, quickly entering the cool shadows of the forest before descending into the valley.

The atmosphere changed instantly - the blustery wind dropped and the canopy of trees closed overhead, the gloom as pervasive as the notable chill.

The whole episode with Hannah seemed more and more surreal by the second. Why had their paths crossed after all these years? And a spiritual healer? She didn't know people did that kind of thing. How did Hannah earn a living? And it was odd about her husband – obviously she hadn't wanted to talk about him, quickly closing off the avenue of conversation. And then there was the moment she'd realised Lauren was staying out here - as if her hair had suddenly crawled with lice.

Without warning the lane dipped sharply, and somewhat distracted, Lauren's reactions were delayed. The car hit the cobbled ford too quickly. Water sprayed the windows on both sides, rain showered off overhanging branches, and in that instant she was blinded. Slamming on the brakes, she grimaced at the sound of a bang underneath, flicked on the wipers and swerved across the lane all inside of a split second. The gateposts to the Grange reared up alarmingly fast as the back end of the car snaked and wobbled. But there was no avoiding the crunch, as unceremoniously it rammed into one of the posts, and metal collided with stone.

"Shit!"

She parked by the cottage door and got out to inspect the damage. A v-shaped dent marked the front panel on the passenger side, and the plaster on the gatepost was quite noticeably cracked.

An image of Lord Landgrave looking down at her from the red leather interior of his car, flashed before her eyes. *And you are?*

"Oh God, no!"

Her glance flicked from the Mini to the pillar and back again. It hardly took Hércule Poirot to work out who'd done it. What if Landgrave drove back this way and noticed? Bloody hell, what to do? Should she walk up to the house and tell someone? Maybe no one would notice, though? And had more serious damage been done to her car when she hit the ford? Oh, God...

The tender point between her heart and solar plexus, where reputedly the soul lay, lurched as if she was a dancer wobbling on a tightrope. For a moment the earth tilted on its axis and she held onto the side of the car. All roads, it seemed, had led to this place. To here and now. To a kind of dead end, back-to-the wall situation. There was no money to pay for this, no way out, no solution, no way out...no way out...

Sebastian's face appeared unbidden - the eyes that on occasion had gazed at her with such longing, increasingly shark-blank. *How dare you compare your filthy past with my beautiful wholesome daughter! She's nothing like you...*

When she'd walked out, because she had to, it had been with almost nothing to her name: a suitcase in the back of the car, an overnight bag, a laptop and a phone.

All around, raindrops sparkled in branches, shot through with prisms of light. They bobbed, glistened and flashed like the silvery dew in hedgerow cobwebs, and the strange feeling of magnetic disorientation experienced earlier, struck her anew. Exactly as had happened yesterday and again that morning, there was a blurring of colours as if standing too close to a painting. What was it about this place? It seemed magical, unworldly, and unpredictable...dangerously so...

After Hannah had been unable to disguise her dismay when Lauren told her where she was staying, she'd had to ask what she meant. The answer had been almost as vague as the one about her husband – just something about the land itself, that it was haunted, and had a reputation over the years for public hangings. Many had been at the crossroads by Fiddlers Elbow, some allegedly on Nine

Rings Hill. There'd also been various stories over the years about hikers cutting short trips they'd not wanted to speak about later.

'It's not a good place," Hannah had said, avoiding eye contact. 'There's an old mill there that had a really bad feel about it. I had to turn back… Well, just be careful, that's all.'

The scenery zoomed in and out of focus, as she held onto the side of the car.

Oh God, I feel so sick and dizzy. What's going on?

She focused on breathing steadily – in and out, in and out - and on the absolute silence of the valley. There wasn't a sigh of air. Not a sound from the woods behind the cottage, which shimmered in a bluish haze. Just the occasional drip of rainwater from the trees.

Gradually, the dizziness began to wear off, and the colours separated into distinct shapes again. It was to step back from the painting and once more see it clearly. Aware now of how cold she was, Lauren snapped out of the trance and went to open the car boot. It must surely be two o'clock!

In the end, Tyler Moody didn't turn up until late afternoon. By then Lauren had stripped the bed and bagged the musty sheets up for Glynis. After remaking it with the newly purchased sleeping bag, army blankets and pillow, she left the fan heater running in the bedroom and switched on the electric fire. Feeling almost drugged with tiredness, she then filled a hot water bottle and popped it into the sleeping bag before making a late lunch. As soon as Tyler had fixed the boiler she planned a soak in the bath and an early night. No one could function well without sleep and the last few days had been off the scale with stress.

As the afternoon darkened, however, she began to feel agitated. He *was* going to turn up, wasn't he? He had to! And what to do about the damaged gatepost? Mention it to him? Maybe he wouldn't notice. Who cared about a teeny bit of cracked plaster, anyway? It would be nothing to people like the Landgraves, but could leave her absolutely penniless if she 'fessed up. She'd end up sleeping in the car. *Oh, God....* Could she get away with it? Indecision nagged away. And what if the prowler came back? Ought she to mention that, as well? What did you do when you didn't know what to do? It seemed impossible at the moment to make even the simplest of decisions, to put any rational thoughts together. In fact, it was an effort to go through the motions of each day and take care of the most basic of needs. When had she last even had a shower? Two days? Three?

She sat by the fire, setting down a cup of camomile on the hearth, and stared into the orange glow of the electric bars. On the periphery of her vision shadows flitted across the walls, but she barely noticed. How quickly and seamlessly the resident ghosts had crossed the veil between worlds. Her eyelids were weighing heavily. What could she do? What could she do about any of this?

Her head lolled, but in a camera flash of white light she was immediately jolted awake again. A second. Had it been a second? Or an hour?

An owl hooted from woods far away. Dusk was closing in rapidly and another night was coming up. Wasn't Tyler Moody coming, then?

There's an old mill that had a really bad feel about it!

I once went walking there...had to turn back!

Was the man at the mill a petty criminal hiding out in

the sticks? What about the other faces at the window?

A fresh belt of rain blew across the glass, the bars of the fire cranked, and dead leaves shuffled around the door. Unable to keep her eyes open, Lauren's head dropped forwards. Oh no, it was going to happen again! And she couldn't stop it.

Mustn't fall asleep… don't… mustn't…

Her fingers clutched at the arms of the chair but it was too late - the dark lap and swell of the lake was pulling her down, down and down, into its nightmare. Until once more she found herself on the lane outside, as starkly detailed and real as it had been that morning. Except now it was dark and the pebbles were glossy and wet. She looked back at the gateposts to the Grange, noting how chalk-white they appeared against the night sky.

And then without any warning she was inside the mill.

Am I a ghost? Is this a dream? I am here, I can see everything…

The flagstone floor was strewn with camp beds, holdalls, cans of pop and empty crisp packets. And a raven-haired man was sitting by a log fire, mesmerised by the flames as rain spattered against his windows like handfuls of shrapnel. A draught whistled through a broken pane, water dripped through gaps in the roof, and damp crept into walls prised apart by ivy. But she found herself gravitating towards what she instinctively knew was there - a ladder leading down to the basement. She didn't want to go there, did not want to drop into the cellar that reeked of cold, wet earth…dark, dark, dark… full of crates, sacks, and boxes…

"No, no, no!"

A sharp rap on the kitchen window brought her out of sleep so fast she jumped clean off the chair.

"What the fuck? Where am I?"

A face was squashed close to the window, peering in through cupped hands.

Her heart was hammering. It took a moment.

And then whoever it was moved swiftly to the door and began to bang on it without stopping.

***

CHAPTER EIGHT

There was almost no preamble. Tyler Moody walked straight through the kitchen to the boiler with barely a word.

Lauren sat waiting while he tutted, swore and clattered around in the hall. The likeness between him and the man at the mill was striking. Although Tyler was considerably older, they possessed the same wiriness about them, quickness of movement, and the kind of piercing observation associated with one permanently on guard. This was not a routine farmer, living in harmony with nature and the surety of its clock. This was a man ready to vanish inside of a second. And like the one at the mill, he seemed to be waiting...always waiting...but for what? Or who?

Lauren crossed her fingers he'd be able to get the heating going. Her breath misted on the air and she was chilled to the marrow. Even her hair smelled of mildew. She looked at her hands and realised they were a faint shade of blue. How did you get your money back from people like the Moodys?

Oh, please let him fix it! God and all the angels, please let me have hot water!

If it didn't work there'd be no option - a confrontation would be inevitable. And she was just psyching herself up for that when suddenly there was a 'boom', and the whole cottage seemed to jump with the shock of it.

"Stupid bitch!" Tyler said, stalking over to the front door. "Got a stupid wife. You do have to turn the bloody thing on, isn't it?"

Her hands flew to her face. "Oh, no! Really? I'm so sorry, I never looked. And I didn't like to touch it. I'm not good with things like–"

"I didn't say you. I said my wife. You're not my wife."

"No, I know but–"

"Anyhow, it'll work fine now. Just press the plus or minus sign either side of the main switch. Need me to show you?"

"No thanks, I'll work it out. Thank you."

"See you then." "Erm, Tyler?"

He had his back to her, hand on the door handle ready to leave.

"Sorry, but I just wondered – does this cottage belong to your farm or D'Avranches Grange? Only I had a bit of an–"

A shadow was floating over the doorway as he turned around to face her. Was someone else lurking there or was it a trick of the light?

"Belongs with the farm. This was a farm cottage, see?"

She frowned, trying not to look at the dark shape hovering over his head. Its movements seemed to be independent from his!

"But the farm's on the D'Avranches Estate."

He sighed audibly. "We're tenant farmers, isn't it?"

He'd assessed her to be as thick as his wife. Still, it wasn't always a bad thing to be under-estimated.

What kind of tenant farmers are you without livestock or crops? "Ah, I see."

"Glynis had the genius idea she'd earn herself a bit of money. Went and rented the cottage out."

She nodded. And maybe they'd fought about that? Tyler didn't want her here anymore than the man at the mill did.

"By the way, I meant to ask Glynis this morning about walking in the woods at the back here. I'd like to see the lake. Was there an old village in the grounds - Groom Lake Village? Do you think they'd mind up at the house if I went exploring or–?"

Tyler's eyes flashed to black. "Well now, I wouldn't advise that. I wouldn't advise that at all."

"Oh, okay. Sorry, it's just that I came here on the understanding there were lots of local walks."

"And there are. Lots. Just not in these private woods. There's a wire fence around the garden perimeter. That's your boundary. Glynis should have said."

His stare was unflinching, and although she kept her focus firmly on his face it was impossible not to notice the hooded black shape begin to separate itself from the shadows and ooze like an oil slick over the threshold. The light from the lamp on the kitchen table flickered and dimmed. And incrementally the room darkened.

"All right. Seems a shame, though. It would have been nice to see the lake."

The sinews in his face tightened. "Best to stay out of these woods. It's set with traps for a start."

"Traps?"

"For game."

"Okay, well that would be sensible, then. I just

thought, with the cottage being… Oh, it's okay."

His stare bored into her for a few moments longer, then seemingly satisfied she was dealt with, he was about to turn back to the door when the words flew from her mouth.

"I found other walks. I went up to the castle yesterday, actually. There's a footpath up there just past your drive. That's one reason I wanted to use the woods, you know - as a shortcut rather than–"

"What did you do that for?"

"Sorry?"

"Nobody goes up there. It's private land."

"No, there's a right of way–"

"Only to a point. The hill itself is private land."

"I didn't know that. It says on the ordinance survey map there's a public right of way."

"The castle ruins aren't safe, either. Story goes a man disappeared from there a few years back. Likely he slipped and fell over the edge. Into the ravine."

"Really?"

"No safety barriers up there."

Recalling the sheer cliff face, she asked, "Did they find him?"

"No, never came back. There are other castles to go and see - ones that have railings and steps. Those would be best for young ladies. Plenty of castles around here to go to - you'll see more along these borders than anywhere else in the world."

"Romans pushing back the Celts and Druids?" *Why did I say that? Where did that come from?*

"English pushing back the Welsh more like."

"Yes."

She couldn't say why - maybe it was because he'd

mentioned someone falling over the edge, but the hooded figures seen up on the hill last night had come to mind. There was a feeling of being in a dungeon - one furnished with trestle tables, and of the low glow of candlelight reflected on wet cobbles. Monks? Or some sort of dark cult? She shivered, aware on one level of the hum of the heating, and on another of a chamber as black as pitch, deep, deep underground…

"Lots of bloodshed here in olden times," he was saying. "Tens of thousands of deaths. Some say the whole place is haunted and you can still hear the screams."

She shook off the incongruent vision and tried to concentrate on what he was saying, even as the room dipped further into shadow. Hadn't he noticed? The effect was like a dimmer switch.

"And that the man who disappeared was sent mad by what he saw. Panicked and fell to his death probably. Wouldn't be the first time round here."

"No body found?"

Slowly he shook his head. "Deep ravine on the other side. Story goes it's the original abyss. Bottomless pit."

The memory from yesterday evening was replaying over and over - the long line of robed figures walking straight off the edge, the steep somewhat flimsy set of steps, and the yawning orifice cut into the sheer rock face.

"That's horrible."

"Ancient sacrifices back in the day. All hail the dark lord."

Bloody hell, I hope he's joking.

"They believed different things back then, I suppose", she said, trying to keep lightness in her voice. "I bet no one goes up there anymore, anyway - not even Lord Landgrave.

Or the children. I mean, it must belong to the family if it's all private land but there isn't much up there and–?"

"Children? What children?"

An all too familiar rise of heat surfaced in her cheeks. "Um, Glynis said they fostered difficult children."

His jaw tightened another notch.

"Did she indeed? Well, I wouldn't know much about that. Not really any of my business." His unspoken words, '*Or yours*' hung in the air between them.

"No, sorry. I'm just interested in history and I thought this was maybe an ancient family seat or something, and I also thought it was nice they helped those less erm…" Dear God, his face was like thunder and her own was burning. "…fortunate. Okay, well thanks anyway. I'll try to find public footpaths and stick to those."

"I would."

His smile, when it began to twitch at the corners of his mouth, reminded her of the triumph one child had over another when they'd won a game.

"At least I've got a neighbour if I get scared," she said.

He'd been about to leave.

"Oh?"

"Saw him earlier at the mill on the corner. Putting out the bins."

"Charon. You met Charon?"

That his name? He didn't speak, but yes, I think so. Seemed nice. Good to have a name now, anyway."

The terse nod he gave was exactly the same as Charon's, before he exited as quickly and silently as he'd arrived.

Every one of her muscles was taut, and it was only after he'd gone she realised her breath was stuck fast in her chest, and finally let it go Walking over to the open door she peered after him. No truck. No sound of footsteps. He'd vanished as swiftly as a fox in the night.

Behind her, however, the chill of the shadow he'd brought had lingered.

Lauren left the door ajar and turned around. None of this could possibly be real. And yet on a subconscious level, she knew that it was. And that she was alone with an unknown, unseen force. There was no one to help, no living being to hear her, and her question rang out in the hollowness of the room.

"What do you want? Who are you?"

The response was the silence of a pond after a stone's sunk and all the ripples have ceased to chase to the edge - the absolute silence of a deep and bottomless lake. And it was with a stab to the heart she realised there was more than one. A crowd of figures now moved around the walls in the orange glow of the fire, the hall beyond a well of darkness, the bedroom an unlit cave.

Her whole being froze. Would there be an answer? Would something materialise? Would she die of the shock?

I don't want to see anything…I can't…

"Whoever you are, leave and leave now!"

It was a feeling more than anything else, of a cold black breeze wafting across the room. It seemed to envelop her in a freezing cloud. And she began to pray, loudly, firmly… 'Our Father, who art in heaven. Hallowed be thy name…" The coldness blew against the heat of her face and her heart rate accelerated to near fibrillation. She was going to faint, to die. Couldn't breathe. "Thy kingdom come, thy will be done…"

What did it want? What could it do?

She kept her eyes squeezed shut, the prayer consistent,

her one happy, pure memory to the fore - a day on the beach in the sun, a child splashing in a sparkling ocean.

And then it was gone. A storm dropped.

She slammed shut the door and drew the curtains.

Already the lamplight had begun to lift.

"Please?" she said to the empty room. "God, do I have any angels, any help? I'm scared, ok? God, please help me? I don't want to go insane."

She sank onto the chair and put her hands over her face. Maybe this was hallucinatory and she was finally going mad? Talking to an empty room! Sobs burst out of her. She never usually even cried. Was known for it. 'Lauren never cries, never gets upset…' Some had even tried to push her, to make her crack - like Sebastian - and still she hadn't. She would not fracture, would not break. Couldn't because…

Had the darkness she always knew was there, finally come for her? Dry-eyed, she held now onto the arms of the chair, staring straight ahead. It felt, she thought, as if an invisible line had been crossed. And nothing was real anymore.

***

Chapter Nine

Every light was on. All the heaters were on. And the bathroom was full of lavender scented steam as she lay back in a tub full of boiling hot bubbles. The tap dripped periodically and behind the flowery blind, rain lashed against the window.

As the rainstorm intensified, she reassured herself repeatedly that the door was locked and bolted. All would be well tonight, all safe. No one could get in.

Except for the shadows.

Glancing at the small mirror-fronted bathroom cabinet through the steam, she half expected to see a hooded figure staring back, and firmly shut out the thought. There was good and bad in the known world - dark and light - so surely that also applied to the unknown one? You could close the door on unwanted guests just the same...couldn't you?

She sank deeper into the hot water, relaxing by degrees. The creature comfort helped. But she couldn't stay in this cottage. It wasn't the kind of break she'd envisaged, hardly conducive to reflecting on why she'd always allowed herself to be treated so badly. All right, she acknowledged – more than treated badly - abused emotionally, physically and psychologically. And now she was broke, unemployed, had no family, and had lost touch with friends. Everything, her entire world, had become dependent on Sebastian.

She closed her eyes. Well, the past was gone. Now there was only today. Zero point. So what practical options were there? The few friends she'd had pre-Sebastian, had families, jobs, and lives that were full. She couldn't go bothering them. There'd been one in particular, Pauline - they'd worked together at a private clinic in London. A memory stirred, of an Italian count in a full length fur coat who'd walked straight into Theatres while his wife was being operated on. She and Pauline had told him no, it was a sterile area, but assuming they could be bought off he'd dropped a few fifty pound notes on the desk and walked right on in. As if they were nothing. The incident had bonded them. But the second she recalled it, and the night out in Camden afterwards, in rolled the rubber and diesel smell of the London Underground. And all the feelings of claustrophobia and panic that came with being deep under the earth.

Underground… Why was she thinking of being underground? The odd scene that had come to mind while Tyler was here, of hooded figures sitting mutely at trestle tables in the darkness of a dungeon, flashed before her and she quickly suppressed the unsettling images. Was that something Tyler was involved in? Something connected to the ethereal figures she'd seen on the hill? Nothing quite pieced together, she could make no sense of it, and her brain was growing tired. You could overthink, she concluded. And she could think no more.

What happened next was fast. Maybe it was the lulling effect of the rain and the slow-drip of the tap. But at the point of dozing off she sank through the ether as surely as if claimed by quicksand. The experience was both brief and jarring, with no time to stop it. And once again she was outside of her own body in a bizarre lucid dream.

This is no dream, Lauren.

I know that…

Lauren, it's not a dream!

This time, however, and it was extremely disconcerting, there was a sense of seeing through the eyes of a man. He seemed au-fait with his surroundings, footsteps purposeful - echoing on smooth, rounded cobbles – as he walked along a gloomy corridor in the damp icy chill of somewhere below ground.

Muffled voices were coming from overhead, a hum of life, like a party being held several floors above a basement flat. Down here, though, it was empty - a vacuous tomb – dimly lit by oil lamps on sconces that threw a dull sulphur glow across the far walls. It had the look of a cathedral, with cloisters, ante-rooms and altars; a vague outline of overhead galleries just visible in the yellowish half-light.

The man was agitated, fingers pressing into the palms of his hands, as he fixed determinedly on his destination. He looked neither left nor right, knowing the way yet seemingly at odds with himself. Nervous, she realised. The frisson of his energy was hers, as the shifting of shrouded shades now rose in a mass of shadows from hidden pews. Clustering around him they began to follow, and her heart clenched.

He knows they're here…is hurrying away…

Now she could see where he was heading. Embedded in the cobbles at the far end, in the darkest section of the main chamber, was a gleam of iron work, a manhole cover. He hurried towards it and slid back the lid. It took effort, his breath laboured, the noise as the iron slab was dragged over the cobbles, heavy and grating. Sparsely lit by further oil lamps, a flight of steps that plunged deep into the earth was revealed, at which point the man quickly turned around and began to descend.

And then hesitated.

He held onto the upper rungs and looked down.

In a hair's breadth of a moment his heartbeat had suddenly escalated to that of a captured bird. An abrupt change had swept over him. He was not himself, seemed in the grip of deep unease as he stared down. He was late, expected…yet today he was unaccountably afraid.

The staircase appeared to descend into a dungeon, lamps all the way down, down and down…for it seemed there was no end to the steps…and she knew at once that many men, for they were all men, had stood in exactly the same spot and been too frightened to continue. Yet he had done this so many times before.

Come on, what's wrong with you, old chap?

A bitter chill emanated from below as if the lid from a long closed casket had been opened, and the faint but distinctly funereal sound of organ music drifted up: a deeply sombre dirge conjuring feelings of wretched grief and black despair.

I can't go down there!

It sounded as if a ceremony or service was about to begin, the organist repeating the introduction, waiting… and waiting…as if for a tardy bride… While several floors above a rowdy event was taking place. All normal. All civilised.

He looked up.

And then down again.

Aware now, profoundly aware, that something shocking

and unexpected was about to happen, and that it would be through this man's eyes – the man whose hands were now visibly shaking, whose brow was wet with perspiration, Lauren told herself to come out of the dream.

Whatever's happening I don't like it. I want to come out.

The water was cooling. Goose pimples rose on her arms.

Come out of the dream.

It was like swimming up to the surface of a black pond, of being able to see a glimmer of sunlight but never quite reaching it

"Lauren, wake up!"

Alas, this time she couldn't.

***

Chapter Ten

As he descends, each step is a dull clang on iron rungs, and an extra layer of darkness closes in overhead as if to seal his decision. Halfway down he pauses again, holding onto the rail. There is something about the sulphuric glow and the damp glistening like sweat on the stone walls... And then he shakes his head and continues. Perhaps he's a little ill this evening, not his usual self?

The men waiting for him are dressed in black hooded robes with only the lower parts of their faces showing. They sit at a long table in the shape of a cross, which is covered in red cloths and set with goblets. At the centre of the table is a menorah - the only form of light in what closely resembles a tomb. The air is stale and the atmosphere oppressive, the deathly hush broken only by the organ playing mournfully in the background. He tries to draw full breath but his lungs are heavy, leaden, as he walks to the head of the table and takes his place.

When finally the organ ceases and all heads bow, he draws to him a leather bound tome penned with ancient script, already laid out at the correct page. The words are familiar, almost boring so often have they been recited. He opens his mouth to speak, expecting to hear the rich resonant bass of his own voice, that all will function perfectly well, his unease merely arbitrary.

"We m…m…meet this day to…to…to… commemorate the death of our most wise and per…per…perfect master, not as…not as…not as…"

He pauses. Every word he utters is a highly disconcerting phone echo, the significance of each one magnified and amplified, resounding through his very soul. He is hearing them as if for the first time, processing them, the same words he's used so many times before. But now, suddenly and profoundly, they have taken on a completely different meaning.

Around him, shoulders stiffen in the penumbra of shadows cast long by the menorah. Surrounding the assembly, the walls are the same smooth stone as the chambers above, the only difference an earthy smell, and the sound of water dripping in the dark recesses of the dungeon.

He attempts to continue. "…not as inspired…or…or…d…d…divine…or…or…"

The realisation of what he's now saying grows like a cancer. It swells into a leaden lump, an embolism blocking his throat, filling his head, blinding him. He has just said Jesus Christ was, 'neither inspired nor divine'.

He's going to be sick.

He clears the ball of phlegm lodged in his oesophagus. And a silent pause stretches into all eternity. No one glances up as he sways and clutches the table. How many times has he led this same ceremony? And for how many years? Yet never once has this happened. Never once have the words struck him in such a way!

He breathes slowly, long deep breaths in deadened air that catches in his throat and stalls each heartbeat. A banging pulse fills his ears.

He must get out, he can't breathe, glances across to the flight of steps... Sees himself running for them, gown flowing behind as he grabs at the rungs.

The drips of the cavern, deep in the bowels of the earth, are each one a jar to the nerves and he swallows down a tidal swell of panic.

Breathe...breathe...breathe...

Until once more he is calm enough to continue with the service.

It is a sombre affair and as the ceremony continues it becomes apparent the room is plunging into hellish darkness, the candlelight too weak to reach even the edges of the table, the stairwell but a faint and distant flicker.

He tells himself, 'this is a play...just a play...just words...' While inside the hollow pit of his stomach, a wretched howl is forming where his soul cowers low. These words have never mattered before. They mean nothing. It's just a ritual, nothing more. That's all. It is all!

But the certainty of truth plunges like a scabbard.

It's been a trick. We've been tricked!

He concludes the ritual with words spoken as if by another. His voice, previously booming and commanding, is now so very far away, warbling and feeble.

"This is indeed a sad day, for we have lost our master. Mourn, weep and cry, for he is gone."

A member of the brethren now stands to ceremoniously extinguish all of the candles in the large menorah, one by one. Until they sit in the total blackness of a pit.

The man draws in his breath, compelling himself to complete the service. It is after all, just a ritual...a play, an act...

"This, the life of our wise and perfect master – is over."

A rolling terror now cloaks him with its agony.

They have just enacted and commemorated the snuffing out of the life of Jesus Christ without once mentioning his name.

The scene ends with the room in deep, silent darkness, and his footsteps echo as he walks from the room, leaving only the stillness of death behind.

***

With each clang of the man's feet on the iron rungs out of the basement, Lauren was lifted out of the dream. Gradually she became aware that despite being fully immersed, it was fading and had not been real. But when she opened her eyes her heart was still hammering as if it was.

Rain was spattering the windows like handfuls of gravel. And for several minutes she lay motionless in the tepid water, focusing on the flowery blind. The man's sickly shock of realisation lingered. What had he done? What kind of terrible choice had he been tricked into? His soul was in anguish.

And who was he? What a strange, strange thing…

Distracted and disturbed, she got out of the bath and quickly towelled herself dry. The heating would be on all night and hopefully the sleeping bag was warm. These dreams were the weirdest she'd ever had, but they were surely just that…dreams?

Another night lay ahead.

"Please, God," she asked out loud. "Please can I just sleep? I'm just so tired. I need oblivion. Total oblivion."

The night, however, was not to be entirely dreamless.

But they were not nightmares. Far from it. And when she woke next morning she was smiling. He, whoever he was, and she could not quite remember, had made her heart dance.

***

Part Two

'In truth, fear is the power of darkness. So if you're afraid of what is about to come upon you, it will overwhelm you, and not one among them will spare you or show you mercy.'

Jesus Christ. The Nag Hammadi Scriptures.

CHAPTER ELEVEN

A low, watery light shone in the puddles on the lane, filtering through skeletal branches blown bare of leaves. And when Lauren opened her eyes next morning it was to the dull, misty greyness of an autumn rapidly turning into winter.

A faint smile still curved her lips as fragments of an erotic dream skittered around the edges of her mind - memories of a man who'd whispered her name, who seemed to know the essence of her far better than she knew herself, who'd probed into the deepest recesses of her being. The smile faded a little. There'd been something embarrassing too, though - something shameful, a side of her personality she hadn't liked very much…and she pushed that feeling, along with an almost overwhelming sense of confusion, away.

All morning, however, while washing, getting dressed and making breakfast, a nagging sense of disquiet persisted and grew. From time to time a peculiar tug in the solar plexus would cause her to stop what she was doing, the sensation like the snag of a tiny fish hook. And an unfamiliar emotion passed across her soul like a wanton storm cloud on a clear day. It was the kind of dread felt by those watching a pond being drained, grimly fixated on a horror that might surface. Because they knew what was down there. They knew but did not want to see, to have it confirmed.

Yet her dream had been a good one, hadn't it?

Once outside her mood lifted. At least it had stopped raining. The boggy earth was strewn with fallen leaves, the trees still dripping like wet coats on a hook. It was one of those days when the sun never truly emerged. Remaining low in the sky it radiated behind a murky veil, its light catching only momentarily in a sparkling raindrop or the silvery outline of a branch. Mist still swathed the valley, and fresh water rushing from every direction sounded as if hundreds of waterfalls were hurtling down from the mountains.

The thought of the mill further up the lane reminded her of the waking dream - of being inside the place, the smell of mould and dank earth, the draught whistling through cracked glass, and the dark dripping cellar. Did the man, Charon, live alone? Who were the shadowy figures seen behind the darkened windows yesterday? Poachers? Squatters? Would that explain the intruder? Maybe what they had to hide was as simple as that? A lot could be explained away as not hugely abnormal, she told herself – ghosts of the past, a dilapidated building housing petty criminals, a bickering couple at a farm? And Hannah's warnings about the area weren't really based on anything other than a morbid history of hangings, were they?

There really was nothing to be afraid of, she reasoned, other than fear itself: the power of the unknown, the unseen. Absolutely everything could be rationalised, even her own sensitivity. There'd be an explanation for that too, such as energy and frequency - she'd been in low spirits and had come to a place like this!

One story Hannah mentioned had been of a horse thief who'd been strung up at the crossroads by Fiddlers Elbow.

It was said he still banged on the inn door after closing time, spooking out the publican and his wife as they lay in bed, which was probably why it was now deserted. Who knew? She recalled the old man walking down the lane towards her on that first evening in the rain. One minute he was there, the next not. Hannah had been referring to a haunted past, that was all. The British Isles was full of spooks. Yet the cloud passing behind her eyes had informed otherwise - Hannah had badly wanted to say more, instead pressing Lauren to take her card and to phone if ever she needed anything. She was a sensitive, who picked up energies more than most, so of course she felt uncomfortable.

The dead couldn't hurt you though, could they?

Lauren eyed the woods behind the cottage. Tyler had gone to such lengths to scare her off. Was it all about poaching? Did the Landgrave family really care about that? And besides, if she stuck to the path there surely wasn't much to worry about: traps would be obvious. There was the strongest pull to go and look, the cool stillness enticing. And the longer she stood there the more powerful the draw.

I can't come all this way and not see the lake. They're just woods... Trees... And no one's around. Tyler won't even know...

Besides, it was time to face her fears and sort out her life. She was here for a reason, and more and more it was beginning to feel like something was waiting to be dredged up and acknowledged. But what? She hesitated. D'Avranches Grange Woods was beckoning – a cool, private place for deep contemplation - and the yearning to sit beside the lake and gaze into it, was irresistible. Would it look the same as it had in the dream she could still remember? She began to walk towards it.

Maybe it's me, she was thinking. I can't change those who hurt me but I can change myself. My path wouldn't have been taken by Pauline, for example. She saw straight through Sebastian, and he wasn't the first.

So what inside of me needs to change? How? What do I need to know? Do I trust too easily? All the wrong ones? Why? For God's sake I have to work this out. There's no one to pick me up if I fall again. No one.

Absorbed by introspection, she was soon beyond the wire netting surrounding the cottage garden, and marching rapidly towards the woods.

Markedly different from the trees covering the surrounding hills, this was a regimental pine forest with a silent ashen interior, and on crossing the threshold, for a fragment of a second, another unsettling feeling of déjà-vu passed over her. Skeins of mist hovered among the tree trunks. She paused briefly. And then stepped inside.

The most noticeable thing was the total absence of sound. It hit her like a wall of pressure. No birds sang and no creatures scurried in the undergrowth. The second thing was a hollow feeling of abject loneliness. Not simply alone. But lonely. Abandoned. Neglected. Not cared about. And with every step along the path that sense of separation increased. She kept on walking, putting the empty feeling down to delayed grief, tamping down the thought that while she was here other people were living full and happy lives. But the terrible sense of despair and hopelessness grew and grew, until eventually it became unbearable and she began to cry.

Lauren never cries, never gets upset.

Further into the woods and the early optimism of

daylight began to dim; and gradually, creeping upon her so stealthily she barely noticed at first, she became conscious of whispering - a silken, busy chatter. It seemed to be coming from within the woods, from among the trees. Realising it was getting louder, more insistent, and had probably been going on for a while, she came to a halt, stopped crying and held her breath.

But there was nothing. All was still and deathly quiet. She began to walk again, the dull plodding of her footsteps on mud now the only sound. From time to time she shot a glance from left to right, half expecting to see the spectres of her dream rising from the undergrowth.

Don't be ridiculous. Don't be silly.

Yet there was most definitely an unnerving sense of being watched, and an awareness that the whispering had now recommenced, but she pushed all of that away and kept determinedly on. The path seemed vaguely familiar, one seen before, known to her, as it wound ever deeper into the core of the forest. From the dream? Was that why? Had that been a premonition? She had to know...Obviously the deeper in the darker it would be, she told herself. Or was a belt of rain sweeping in again? The light was going.

Yet it was early morning.

She stopped to look up at the sky, instantly sensing a hissing recoil, as if the ghosts of yesteryear who'd been coming ever closer, now fell away. She stood stone still, straining to hear. No, it must have been a trick of the mind. There was no one here, no movements between the gaps in the trees, and nothing emerging out of the mist. It was just a memory, and a memory of a dream at that. She peered upwards - these trees had grown tall of spine, the tops spiking into the clouds, trunks bare of branches and needles. It was not a dense forest, so why was it so dark? And the sky was…white… a white haze…no rain clouds, no storm…

She glanced in the direction of what she knew to be the centre, to where the lake lay. How utterly black it was!

The essence of the forest seemed to hold its breath, and the catching feeling in her solar plexus happened again, the snag of a fish hook. She put her hands over the tender place, comforting herself with her own body warmth. No matter the logic, the amount of reasoning or potential explanations, instinct was instinct, as raw and honest as that of a wild animal. And there was something horribly off-kilter in these woods. It was *not* her imagination.

As she stood there, motionless, her heart suddenly picked up a beat. Every nerve fired.

Something's coming!

And no sooner had that thought formed when rapid footsteps pounded on the path behind.

She leapt around.

A waft of freezing air brushed her face as if someone had just run past. A swirl of dust and a flutter of stray leaves blew across the path in a freak gust, and she stared at the empty space. This was an exact replay of what had happened in the dream.

A replay? A ghostly replay? What had happened in these woods?

As if by way of an answer, a burst of laughter echoed from beyond the tree line and she steeled herself. What the hell was this?

Not a dream, Lauren. This is not a dream!

She was almost at the centre. Almost at the lake. Static crackled in the air like a vintage film. Would the little girl be there, barring the path, the child in the blue raincoat and flowery wellingtons?

She must get to the lake. And after that she'd go. It was just the need to see it, to check if it was the same as the dream...

But what then, Lauren? What if it is? How will you explain that away?

Long before she rounded the last corner of the magnetic maze, however, Groom Lake reared into her mind's eye and lodged there until she could think of nothing else.

Must see the lake...I just want to see it... just once! And then I'll know.

Her pace quickened. A distant scream rent the air, a cry that could be a screech owl or a hunted creature caught in a trap. She could not be sure because there were other noises, too. The ones who whispered had grown imperceptibly bolder; here and there came the pulsing breath of a horse at a gallop, or the pounding of feet. And the closer she drew to the lake, the more the trees seemed to shrivel and wither - the branches gnarled and barren - shrinking back into roots.

Faster and faster she walked, hurrying now, until finally Groom Lake was before her. It appeared all at once, almost triumphantly, disgusting to the eye. But this time there was no child to block the view and she could see it clearly.

Groom Lake, a still and lifeless circular pond, was ink black. Not a single pine tree was reflected on its surface and no breeze produced a ripple. There it sat, squat as a toad and thick as oil, the air old and sour like a bad drain.

At last...

***

CHAPTER TWELVE

Without pausing she continued straight to the edge, despite the mud that tugged and sucked at her feet like quicksand. She had to reach the rim, and only ground to a halt when it wasn't possible to get any closer and water surged over her boots.

The pool was deep and stagnant, her reflection dull. For several moments she swayed back and forth like a pendulum, rooted in the quagmire. Not a breath of air stirred the surface of the water, which mirrored nothing but herself. Mesmerised, unable to help leaning over, she peered in. Way down in the inky depths there was movement. Was something down there? Perhaps it was the towering trees causing an illusion? Yet the surface was opaque and utterly devoid of light. And there wasn't the faintest breeze.

Dizzy, sleepy, she resisted the overwhelming compulsion to topple forward, to fall in, and be claimed. The atmosphere felt charged as if once again a storm was brewing, the woods swathed in a bluish haze. Her limbs were leaden and it was an effort to wrench her attention away, to focus on what had been obscured in the dream - not just the lake but what lay directly across from it: D'Avranches Grange.

The house had a certain presence, hunkering wide and low in the belly of the woods with fleeting glimpses of

Woodsay Castle high above. Built in grey stone, it was only partially hidden by the leafless trees, and would probably not be visible at all in summer. Two wings spread out from either side of a pointed archway in the middle, which led through to a courtyard at the back. She squinted through a veil of mist. What a strange design. Neither Romanesque nor Gothic, the house was an enigma. Above the archway an immense oculus formed a rose window, which was inset into a long wall connecting the two wings. Divided by stone mullions and bars, the oculus held radiating stone spokes like a wheel, reminiscent of something found on a cathedral rather than a country home. Its fairy tale beauty was enchanting.

'There,' she thought vaguely – 'the fairy tale quality again...'

Along the length of both wings all the leaded windows were pointed arches set into thick stone walls, with those on the ground floor opening onto expansive lawns.

She became lost in thought. *Such opulence, such exquisite attention to detail and comfort.*

Not one of the long windows, however, caught the light, due to a balustrade of pillars. Nor, from this angle, were there any visible doors - no grand porch or entrance of any kind. She frowned, realising it was becoming increasingly difficult to stay awake, or indeed to concentrate on anything at all. In fact, the house seemed to merge with the scenery, to shimmer like an optical illusion, and a low hum was building, the sound a swarm of bees. Far away in the recess of her mind there was a feeling she'd heard the hum before, but could not think where.

Maybe, she thought, the house was built around the courtyard and the entrances would be from within that?

Was it a hunting lodge of some kind? It didn't look like a standard stately home, lacking a family church or formal gardens; and the architecture was a jumble of styles. Perhaps it was medieval, or had once been a monastery? It looked like it could have been, with cloisters and pillars, and its proximity to the woods, river and fields beyond....Except for the mood...

The energy of the place wasn't peaceful. Something about it jarred. It sapped the colours and vibrancy from everything around it, and when the pale low sun washed briefly across the tops of the distant hills, it failed to lift the sombre gloom from the lawns. Move the focus of the eye to its outer edge and it became a void, a black hole where a jigsaw piece should be - non-existent.

Lauren continued to survey D'Avranches Grange for a long time, even as her back chilled and a fine rain began to blow in from the moors. Mud oozed up her boots as she sank deeper, but she found the more she looked the more she saw. It was a damp chilly morning but there wasn't any smoke coiling from the chimneys. And there were no lights on in the upstairs rooms. In fact, for all the world it looked unoccupied. Yet Lord Landgrave had driven in just yesterday. And what about the young girl? Well maybe, she reasoned, that part of the dream hadn't been a premonition at all, but just a dream and nothing more?

Yet Glynis had said they looked after children.

So who cleaned and cooked for the family? That was a massive pile and people like that didn't scrub their own bathtubs. There was no one else around here apart from Charon at the mill. Maybe their servants lived in? Yet the big house was as quiet as a graveyard, without a single sign of life either within or without.

No life…we're just waiting…waiting…and waiting…

A sudden coldness spread across her back and she looked down to see a shivery ripple travel across the surface of the water, as if a large fish swam below. The atmosphere was becoming incrementally more oppressive, both the low hum and sulphur smell increasing. Time to set back. This was nothing but a neglected pond in a lifeless wood, she told herself. So she'd seen it in a dream! So what? Lots of people had out of body experiences. What could she possibly have thought was so special about it?

Yet it lured her then, as a mirror lures the vain. And against all rationale or free will, oblivious to the mud pulling at her boots, she stared into it once more… It was just a stupid puddle of water…and stooped over.

This time the effect was that of a scrying mirror. Her image wavered in the water's dark reflection, no shaft of light permeating the matte of its oil-slick surface. Yet she could see herself so clearly. How extraordinary!

Long fair hair framed an elfin face and she saw now what Sebastian had seen, and many others before him: eyes the colour of a turquoise lagoon, fair hair that was almost white – mermaid colouring he used to say – an ethereal, fay appearance. Not the kind of looks people forgot.

I shouldn't be alone.

I deserve so much more.

A great longing now clutched her soul. It squeezed her heart and wrenched out tears as before her eyes she saw what she could have had – steel strong arms around her waist, the citrus, musky, leathery scent of masculine skin, the power of a twin flame gently, oh so gently, pushing her back onto…pillows…

Pillows…a soft downy bed, leaded windows and a starry

night sky…

Mesmerised she gazed intensely into the murky depths of the lake, leaning further and further forwards. How come she could see this playing out - down there on the bottom of the lake, so deep? Her heart ached, yearned. She had been so alone. Was this the future?

Too late, something swelled, stirred, and then broke though the film.

She reeled back. The breath caught in her chest.

Whatever it was had jumped out of the water.

***

CHAPTER THIRTEEN

"Hello, Lauren," said a male voice inside her head.

Her first thought was demonic possession. She clutched at her temples. Entities could walk into people, she'd read about it. Drug users or those actively inviting in the unknown had become infested, adopting totally different characters. It was known about, documented, witnessed since time immemorial…*Oh my God!*

But could it happen by staring into a dark mirror, be it glass, crystal or water? Because there was no doubt something terrible had taken hold! Nor was it wasting time. A web of fine probes was already fanning out rapidly - tapping into thoughts, experiences and personal moments. Her brain crawled with the alien presence, its tentacles reaching into the deepest fibres of her being, as one by one every mortifying regret was replayed and magnified all the way back to childhood.

Insecurities, suppressed fears and unhealed traumas surged to the surface in a rush of humiliation. In one hit she saw the lie she'd told her best friend in school, and how that girl had known she was lying, the friendship forever spoiled. She saw herself cheating at an exam she later won a prize for; watched her teenage self have cheap sex with a boy who despised her; and in painful slow motion relived the wedding she should never have had, to a man she didn't love. Her insides contorted with the agony of guilt and shame. And the rapid playback didn't abate until Sebastian had mimicked her with a whiny voice she didn't know she had; finally ending with the image of the young girl in her dream – the one who'd blocked the path to the lake.

The whole episode had taken less than a second, had been a flash, a singular moment. And then it stopped dead, a computer all out of bytes. She stood swaying, in shock. Whatever the presence inside her was, it had just osmotically soaked up the sum total of her life and spewed it back. All the bad things. All the worst memories – the ones no one would ever want to recall or repeat – in a heartbeat.

She found she couldn't move.

What was happening to her? All her thoughts collided in chaos. It was impossible to look away from the lake, to turn her head or move her feet. And as she stood transfixed, macabre images began to take form in its black depths. They were breaking away from the mud and murk, just as the shadows in the forest had done, to take their place in a grim theatre of dance.

She watched in mesmerised horror, as in the dull reflection corpses now dangled from nooses. Starlight glittered overhead and torch flames flickered and darted among the trees. A shout ripped through the air and horses hooves thundered along the paths from every direction. Behind, there was a quick crepuscular rustle of a long, silk dress; and then the rapid pant of someone running.

Still she could not tear herself away. She was part of a play, unable to prevent the rapid unfolding of events, as if a book or film had pulled her into its virtual world. A woman in a full length riding habit, with rouge spots on a chalk-powdered face, flew out of the dark mirror of the water, black button eyes glittering with malice. In her hand, a leather crop was raised high above her head, about to be thrashed down…

Flinching as if it was really happening, Lauren finally managed to close her eyes, and yelled, "No! Stop!"

The male presence was mocking. "Hello, Lauren! Would you like a little preview? Come on, you wanted answers."

Her own voice echoed around the dark bowl of her head, plaintive and whingy, causing her to despise herself further. 'Why is this happening to me?' it wailed, 'I'm so alone…'

Stuck fast in the quagmire, her body rocked to and fro. Something else was coming. A faint breeze blew against her face.

"A little preview. Call it a personal gift, or a premonition."

Disturbing images were then propelled into her mind - a film reel she had no choice but to see, to live, to participate in.

"No!"

Yet part of her, a facet barely acknowledged, *did* want to know!

"Yes, yes!"

She was in bed with a man whose face was shrouded in darkness, candlelight flickering on thick stone walls. The sensation was not unpleasant, and again there came a jolt of déjà-vu, the air fragrant with a heady, musky scent. The man was massaging her bare skin, his hands kneading and pummelling, but what was this? The stark white sheets were all smeared. The fact washed over her. A toppled bottle of red wine, probably…?

A sharp pain abruptly stabbed her lip. He was bending over her, tilting his head towards her in the exact same way Sebastian used to. Had that been a bite? Her reactions seemed delayed… And why was he smiling? The kiss that then came was far from gentle. It slammed onto her mouth and fastened hard as iron. He was, she realised, sucking the blood from her, draining it out in great rolling waves. At the point where she could take no more, couldn't speak or breathe and tried to shove him away, he yanked her head back by the hair, dropped further down, and bit the nipples. He bit one and then the other. She gasped as he bit and sucked, and even though she could not see his face she knew it was covered in her blood. Yet despite the pain, desire overruled it all, and it was blinding. Flipping her over, he now pulled her down the ruby-spattered sheets by the legs until he was hard against her, pulled back her head, and then sank sharp pointed teeth straight into her carotid artery.

Life's over….life's over…draining away…

Her heartbeat catapulted to near fibrillation as their bodies now fused with what felt like the excruciating pain of a burning sword inside her.

There were no words… no cries out…just a sensation of floating away, dropping through the ether onto soft, downy pillows…

I've been here before!

And when she opened her eyes again it was to see leaded windows, a star filled night spiked with treetops, and tapestries hanging on the walls.

Yes, been here…

But this time someone was laughing. Gradually she

became more and more aware. There was movement in the candlelight, and robed figures stepping out of the shadows to clap and raise chalices. Not normal people, though. Some had animal masks on, and antlers on their heads…

"Bravo! Well done – superb!"

"No! This isn't real. Stop! Stop now!" She stood panting, reminding herself repeatedly that it wasn't actually happening, that this was a nightmare and there was something terrible and evil about the lake. In the far corners of her mind she instructed herself to say the Lord's Prayer, and somehow the words began to form. "Our Father, who art in heaven…"

His laughter reverberated in waves, coming from every direction, callous and cold. "You loved it, Lauren. You wanted it. You always did."

"No. This is tricks and lies."

Her heart bounced around in her chest as she resumed the Lord's Prayer, citing the words over and over and over. How could it be that the voice was inside her head? How could it be that all her worst memories, shame and guilt, had been invoked? What kind of place was this? She had to get out of here. Fast. And yet her feet were sinking into the mud, boots already swallowed.

Can demons possess water? Is this an energy vortex? Will I die here?

A long time ago, a nurse colleague had told a story about her brother. He'd once played Ouija with a gang of friends. Once. Because afterwards one of the boys had committed suicide. Her brother said they'd all seen a dark shape skittering around the wall before it seemed to choose and settle on that particular boy. He'd been a fearful kind, a depressive who drank too much, and as he left they'd all seen the attachment he took home with him. Why him, though? Why him and not one of the others? There'd been something else she'd said, too. What was it? Something important…

Oh yes, that was right – the boys had offered blood to the unseen forces they hoped to attract. Each had bled their wrist.

Blood!

A low chuckle echoed in the woods, and she sensed the gloomy chill of a dark cloak around her, akin to sitting wet in the shade of a tree on a summer day. A chill blew through to her bones, the light dimmed to fog, the air static.

"Lauren, it's over. You're going under, going down…and no one even cares. What a mess you've made of your life. What a waste of time. You learned nothing. What a joke you are!"

Later, she thought it had been the word, 'joke.' But whatever it was, it propelled her straight out of the trance, and an unknown strength came out of nowhere. Anger first. Rage.

"I'm not afraid of you, you nasty bastard. Get the fuck out of my head."

"Oops, talking to yourself. Never a good look. Medicine time! Asylum time! No one will believe you, Lauren."

Ignoring the taunting laughter, she forced herself to picture warm sunlight and that one gloriously happy childhood holiday in South Wales, the delight at running into sparkling waves with a bucket and spade. Her heart filled with the bliss of the moment and the words burst out of her, "I am a child of God, the Creator, and I am of the divine light."

Outrage consumed her. There was no question of this happening. How dare he! It! Pulling her stocking feet straight out of the boots, almost comically flailing in her haste, she then bent to pick them up, and sopping with mud, stumbled and fled towards the path out of the woods. Whatever had happened to the boy who'd played Ouija that night, it had been real enough. His personality had changed almost totally. He'd become violent and abusive, been admitted into psychiatric care and eventually overdosed, convinced a legion of demons was following him. That would not happen to her. This was a violation. She had not invited this or offered blood or got drunk. So how in God's name had this happened?

You know! You know!

As she walked, faster and faster, the trees formed an archway overhead as they had driving into the valley the day before – a gloomy tunnel with only the faintest of lights, a dot, at the far end.

My dream. Again, my dream!

Except this really wasn't a dream. In fact, never had life seemed so urgent or so vividly intense. Every beat of her pulse was a shock wave as she then broke into a sprint.

I have to get to the light!

Who could she go to? Anyone? Tyler Moody had warned her out of here on a pretext. Maybe he wasn't the bad guy, after all? There'd been a tiny flicker of concern in his eyes when he'd been laying it on thick yesterday. Maybe it'd been a way of protecting her? Was it possible he knew what this place had been, that the haunting of it was real? And maybe Glynis didn't?

They have no children…

Her stockinged feet pounded the ground, drumming in her ears, just as the ghostly ones had done.

Nearly there, nearly there… The pale grey wash of colour that passed for daylight at the end of the path was within reach, and the closer she got the more her mind began to clear, despite a strong feeling of darkness around her, a coolness that wafted around her back and head. Was he, or it, following her? What…did it stay with her? Was it attached?

Oh, God!

She forced herself to keep focusing ahead, speeding up. Not far now.

And when finally she burst out of the woods a few seconds later, she winged straight round to face the path behind, doubled over with stitch, gasping for breath.

No one there. No one and nothing.

There was something seriously evil about that lake. The whole place, she thought, as she had on the hill that first day, seemed to be locked in the past. Time, a strange concept in itself, seemed to have blurred here, magnetically pulling the soul into a re-enacted game.

"I'm never going to that lake again. Not ever."

The clouds were loaded and about to drown the forest with another fresh load of rain by the look of it. It spattered on the breeze and whipped up flurries of leaves. Straightening now, she hurried over to the cottage and put the key in the door.

How icy it felt on stepping over the threshold!

Shivering, she tugged off the wet socks. Problem was, with money so tight there was little choice but to stay here until she had somewhere else to go - a job, a plan! She took off her sodden coat and went to the bathroom. Every hair on her head seemed to prickle, the skin on her back goosing.

Light. Somewhere there was light and life would be where she'd go today. All she could control was now, not yesterday and not tomorrow. Only now. And the priority was sanity. Lunch out then, she decided. Anywhere as long as it was away from here - lunch in town surrounded by normal people would be good. And on top of that she'd buy a new coat since this one was ruined.

"Enough," she said as she hastily changed her clothes. "Just enough. I deserve better. Why can't good things happen to me like they do for others? I could land a job. Meet someone. Anything!"

And even as an elongated shadow crept around the walls and the bathroom light faltered and flickered, she spoke out loud most emphatically, "I'm not having this anymore. I'm just not. I'm going to change things. I'm going to change my whole life."

***

CHAPTER FOURTEEN

No doubt about it, Owlbury felt totally different than it had the day before. Was it really only yesterday she'd walked along here feeling watched? Only twenty four hours since the ghostly booming of the corn exchange, a market square alive with flapping chickens, and a man in breeches playing the flute on the town hall steps? The shadowy imprints of the past had woven into the town's medieval tapestry.

Today, however, all of that had faded away, leaving an ordinary rain-sodden town with streets full of characterless corporate uniformity. Lauren's footsteps resounded on the cobbles as she walked through the alleyways and past the church railings, half expecting to hear the sound of horses' hooves or whispered gossip from doorways. But there was none. Nor was there any glowering hostility directed towards her. In fact, she blended in, barely noticed.

A couple clad identically in jeans and anoraks held hands in front of a jewellery shop window, the woman pointing to this and that. A man with a bald head and full beard walked out of a shop absorbed with a mobile phone, almost bumping into her. And two elderly women in hats, gloves and long coats stood chatting outside the bakery, the smell of hot pastry wafting on the air. She struggled for a word other than 'normal' but there wasn't one. Normal was what it was. No ghosts. No suspicious glances. The town really had lost its haunting atmosphere, and so had its inhabitants.

Or maybe it was she who'd changed?

In the reflection of a shop window, she caught a glimpse of movement behind her, a dark shape, but could not be sure. Was this something to do with what happened this morning? There was definitely a change, a kind of leaden feeling in her limbs, a chill around her shoulders.

Not possible, surely? It had been a bad, strange place, a trick of the mind. She was not possessed. There was no attachment. *Stop it. No! Enough*!

She began the search for a women's clothes shop, cheered to find an independent store. An old-fashioned bell tinkled as she pushed open the door.

"Can I help you?"

A woman of indeterminable middle age was sitting behind a glass-topped desk sipping coffee, the aroma hanging in the air. The dove grey of both her hair and sweater was broken by a froth of fuchsia at her neck, her reading glasses dangling on a string of metallic beads.

Lauren shook her head. "No, it's all right. I'd just like to look, thanks."

The woman stood up, still clutching the mug. "So do you know what you're looking for? Is it for work or–?"

"I'll probably know when I see it."

"Well, feel free to look around. There's more upstairs."

"Thanks."

"I like the jacket you've picked up, actually. Now that would be gorgeous on you. It only came in last week. Hold it up to your face. There's the mirror."

Feeling a little pushed, Lauren had been inclined to put

what was a patently ridiculous item back on the rail. A long waterproof jacket was what she needed to replace the one she had on, not a glamorous faux fur. But the woman had moved position so she was almost behind her, and aware of the mud she hadn't been able to fully remove from the back of her coat, Lauren duly swung round to face the cheval mirror.

The expression on her face was startled, eyes wide, cheeks flushed; and she knew in that instant and without doubt, that the coat would be hers. The soft black fur was as glossy as a well-fed cat, gleaming under the shop lights. Lauren hugged it to herself, running her hand down its thick warmth. She'd been so, so cold.

"Try it on."

Oh, what the heck?

A minute later it was on. She pulled up the generous lapel and snuggled into it, turning this way and that.

"Oh, you look fabulous."

It certainly did something for her. In fact it was transformational, setting off her trademark white blonde hair. Two rose pink spots flushed her cheeks. She'd forgotten. Had simply forgotten what she looked like.

"Honestly, with you being so slim it's just pure glamour. No one big could wear that and look so elegant."

She walked around a little, pushing her hands deep into the pockets. Actually it would be great over a little black evening dress; and on long romantic country walks… How warm it was! How…

Ridiculous…

"I'll take it."

The owner nodded and helped her out of the coat. "What about a scarf to go with it? Or a new bag?"

Both women eyed a black patent clutch with a silver clasp.

"Hmmm..."

It seemed to leap off the shelf into her hands. To be fair, she thought, a fabulous coat like this would look silly with a tatty, navy shoulder bag. She needed a clutch. In her head she was already wearing a little black dress, being led into a restaurant, slipping off the luxurious jacket. What if she had a night out?

"I'll take it, yes. And then I think I'd better get out of the shop."

"Husband might ask questions?"

Lauren laughed, feeling the peculiar tug inside again - the snag of a fish hook. She would like a husband. Someone to love. Someone who put his arms around her. Someone to laugh with, to hold...

"So that's a hundred and twelve pounds, then. Is it card or cash?"

The roses in her cheeks burned slightly hotter as she took out her purse. There was hardly anything left in the bank. No job. No place to live.

"I'll put the jacket on now, thanks. Only I fell into a puddle this morning."

"Oh no, how awful."

"No, honestly, it was nothing. Just tripped."

For the briefest of moments it felt as if they were play acting, the two of them just saying lines, and that everything was a long way off, somehow disconnected. It didn't last long but she was glad to leave, and as soon as the coat was back on, with the old one in a bag, she walked over to the old black and white inn opposite.

On approach, a frisson of excitement began to play

inside, a fluttering of moths. Anything could happen. Never in her life had she felt so on edge. Things were about to change, and she knew that as surely as a gambler throwing his last dice. One way or the other, everything would switch today.

From within came the low murmur of conversation, and ducking to avoid a low beam she walked up to the bar. She deserved this. One day out. One day of pleasure. Call it a mini holiday. It was just a coat. This was just a lunch. Might as well enjoy!

Behind the bar, bottles were reflected in a mirror, the light from a Tiffany lamp catching the pearlescent shine of her hair against the ebony coat. Eyes were on her, the conversational hum muffled as she scanned the menu. The thought occurred then – what if there was a vacancy? What about getting a job and staying?

The bartender was smiling as she looked up to peruse the blackboard. Another man on one of the bar stools caught her eye and winked.

"Um, yeah. Half a cider please, the um…" God, if only her cheeks didn't flare up so much, giving her nerves away. She indicated the low alcohol option on tap. "Um–"

"You have a think," said the barman, pulling the cider as he looked her up and down. "That's all fresh fish on the board, by the way - came in this morning."

Yesterday she'd scurried past this old pub and seen a dark cavern floating with straw. Today the sloping floorboards were polished, brasses gleamed, lamps aglow. It was a nice ambience, congenial, and she'd just begun to relax when a male voice boomed directly behind.

"I can recommend the lobster ravioli actually. It's incredibly good."

The man who'd spoken had appeared out of nowhere. The door had not sounded and there'd been no waft of cold air from the street. Yet now he was standing close behind, towering over her, chin level with the top of her head.

Shocked by both the sudden proximity and the voice, she glanced over her shoulder.

The glance became a double-take, then a wide-eyed stare. And after that her mind blanked.

***

Chapter Fifteen

He was way more attractive without the reflective sunglasses. Wearing a white shirt that contrasted sharply with the jet curls of his hair, he raised his eyebrows and smiled. A wide, slow smile.

Lord Landgrave's eyes were so dark a brown as to be almost black, glinting now with amusement as she struggled to find the right words. Although quite tall at five foot eight – taller with heeled boots – he dwarfed her, the power of his presence a heady mix of fragrant oils and masculine beauty.

Conversation fell away. There wasn't a single coherent thought in her head as she continued to stare. And the moment was becoming uncomfortable. She must say something, but was unable to form a sentence. Others had started to notice. What to say? What to do? Her mind was in fog, and to make matters worse an annoying blush had begun to suffuse her entire face. Horrified, she realised it was now aflame and quickly turned back to the bartender, realising too late she hadn't actually answered the man. Even her hands were shaking. How utterly embarrassing to have reacted like this!

All eyes were fixed on her, and what was possibly the most interesting bit of entertainment the pub's clientele had witnessed in a very long time.

The blackboard chalked with dishes of the day swam before her. Hot blood burned in her cheeks. God, could she have turned any redder? This was mortifying.

"I'll er…go for that then, please."

"The lobster?"

She nodded. It was sixteen pounds she realised belatedly, rooting for her purse.

"Good choice," said Lord Landgrave. "I'll have the same, thanks."

He smelled of citrus, sandalwood, leather…rain…

"Settle up later if you want," the barman said to Lauren, who was still rummaging in her bag.

"Oh, right. Okay, thank you." She took a sip of cider. Good, it was nice and cold. She took another, then smiling vaguely in Lord Landgrave's direction, moved swiftly away. How excruciating was that? How come she hadn't been able to speak? Her hands were still visibly trembling. It was ludicrous. The man was a bloody aristocrat and at least twenty years older than her. All she had to do was thank him. That was it. All over. Instead she'd turned into a self-conscious schoolgirl picked out by a teacher and jeered by classmates. He'd managed to set her back twenty years.

She looked around. There weren't many empty tables in the pub: one was squeezed up to a wall by the kitchen, another set for a party of six in the bay of the window.

Behind her, too closely, he said, "There are some far nicer ones in the back room."

Again she lost the ability to think straight. The voice – deep and resonant like a finely tuned double bass – tapped into something she could not place. "Oh, I didn't realise. Thank you."

Of course I didn't realise. I've never been here before. Calm down, Lauren. He's a judge and a lord and has a wife. Don't be so stupid.

"There's a fire in there, too. Rather cold today, isn't it? Bit miserable outside."

"Yes. Thanks."

She headed for the back room, keen to put some distance between them. Should she apologise for the gatepost? Had he noticed yet? Did he even recognise her from yesterday in the lane when she'd been wearing a scruffy anorak? Maybe not… Hopefully not.

Even now it was impossible to think of anything intelligent to say. With luck he wouldn't follow her, anyway. Tad awkward! She wandered into what was a totally empty oak-panelled ante-room, choosing a table by the open log fire.

One day I'll laugh about this - the time I made a complete tit out of myself in front of a pub full of smirking middle-aged men. The grown woman who turned beetroot and couldn't string a sentence together!

Her face was still flaming as she set the glass on the table and sat down. Only to see Lord Landgrave duck under the low beam, glass in hand.

Oh, fuck no!

She calmed her breathing, attempting to wrest back some control. She had wished for love, for arms around her, but this was not it. Men like him didn't view women like her as anything other than a cheap, throw-away thrill. They had land, money, and well connected families. She would be nothing, something to laugh about later, or more likely forget ever existed. And yet a chord had been struck deep inside. And he was walking straight over, almost as if the meeting was pre-destined.

Déjà-vu again! It washed through her, leaving behind a feeling of displacement, of being in freefall. The room was fragrant with burning apple wood, centuries of beer and smoke ingrained into its timbers. And as he neared she caught the added scent of citrus and sandalwood.

"Is it cheeky to ask to join you? Only," he indicated the fire. "That looks so inviting."

He was right, she thought, it was cheeky; but in fairness the fire was warm and the rest of the room was parlour cold.

"Um, sure."

Her stomach tied itself into a knot as he took a seat opposite, set down a pint and then rubbed his hands over the flames.

Oh, Lord, what to say to him? What was he doing here anyway? Why would someone like him be buying a lone pub lunch in a dreary wet market town?

He looked over and smiled - a boyish charm offensive. "I'm being an awful pain. Can you ever forgive me? I'm Wil, by the way. Nice to meet you."

"Lauren. Lauren Stafford. But we met yesterday, didn't we?"

He did that thing of frowning and smiling at the same time.

"You're Lord Landgrave. I'm staying at the cottage by the gate..." She'd almost said, 'gatepost' and stopped just in time. Why was he frowning?

"I'm afraid you've made an assumption."

His accent was pure Home Counties, the resonant tone of his voice having a physical impact that jarred the chambers of her heart. It would be doubtful anyone standing before him in the dock would dare answer back.

Her reply sounded feeble, even to her own ears. "I'm sorry, I don't understand. I was in the lane yesterday outside the D'Avranches Estate and you stopped to–"

"Yes, but I'm not Lord Landgrave. I'm simply guesting."

"Oh, I see."

His complexion was absolutely unmarked by time, skin the colour of pale honey, eyes un-creased at the corners. How old was he? She'd thought late forties to early fifties.

He began to slip off the raincoat, the white shirt tight on muscular arms, and briefly she looked away. He was laughing, brushing off raindrops from his hair, which she could now see was streaked with silver.

"The Landgraves are family."

"Oh, I see," she said again.

"I came here a lot when I was growing up. My parents would often be out of the country during holidays. They forgot to arrange something completely one year. Left me standing in the headmaster's office with my suitcase. Good job I've got an uncle."

"You were at boarding school?"

"Correct. So tell me, are you enjoying your holiday in the rain?"

She laughed. "I've been here for two days and it hasn't stopped."

By the time the meals arrived he'd told her he had a company involved in international politics and banking, had just returned from Mauritius and would be here for another week. Until Halloween was over. His family and friends were having a huge party. Enormous fun, apparently - an annual event not to be missed.

And after a second glass of cider she confided she'd

been a nurse and had spent a lot of time in London, stopping dead at the point where she'd met Sebastian. What could she say? That the man had asked, no begged her, to work alongside him in business, but the job had never materialised? Meantime she'd lost her professional footing, most of her friends, and never went anywhere ever again? His gaze flicked briefly to the soft inside part of her wrist as she picked up that second glass. And when she went to the bathroom, she did not need to glance back to know his eyes were taking in the shape of her and the way she moved. Anyone else and she would've kept on walking all the way to the door and flown back to the car. This was a pick-up, a cheap and obvious pick-up in a bar.

Yet she stayed.

The toilet facilities were basic and sobering and she took her time - washing her hands, letting the chilly air breezing in through the small back window caress her face. For sure he must have slept with hundreds of willing women. They doubtless threw themselves at him. No wonder he was so confident and forward. This was madness. All she would think about now was him. His voice chimed with the beat of her pulse, his presence filled her senses, the drowsy hum of background conversation hypnotic.

Holding her hands under the whirring dryer, she looked over the top of it into the mirror, seeing what he might see: a sheen of long ivory hair, aqua eyes and dilated pupils – so huge, abnormally so - mascara slightly smudged from laughing, and red, red lips…bitten…

And I am drunk. And stupid. And foolish.

He watched her walk all the way back again, keeping his gaze firmly on her face, only covertly glancing at her body when she bent to sit down.

You know. I know!

By then, the afternoon had dipped to dusky, rain lashed the windows, and the fire crackled and spat.

Nursing the coffee he'd ordered in her absence, she stared into the flames. He'd picked up the bill. His card lay on top of the invoice in full view. How long since anyone had bought her lunch? Did it matter? One day? Just this once?

"Thank you for this. It's been lovely."

"Not at all. I've enjoyed the company immensely, and I wanted a seat by the fire."

She laughed and took another sip. This whole surreal interlude was coming to a close. Part of her wanted it to last forever, and another to bolt for sobriety.

"I'd love to take you out some time."

She looked away.

"Don't worry, nothing like that – just you know, lunch or tea and cake or something." He held up his hands. "I didn't mean to offend you."

"You haven't. Actually, I'm extremely flattered, thank you." She drained her coffee. "But I'll have to pass. I hope you enjoy the rest of your holiday and thank you. It really has been an unexpected treat."

Standing up, she wobbled slightly and he reached out to steady her by the elbow.

"Are you okay? Another coffee?"

Lauren sat down again. Seriously, two halves of cider with a meal and she was drunk? "No, it's okay. It's just the heat. I'll walk around outside for a while before driving back."

"I can give you a lift?"

"Oh no, it's fine, honestly. And I wouldn't want to leave my car here. Not that anyone would take mine." She laughed.

"I could tail you, to make sure you get back safely?"

"No, really. I've only had two glasses of cider. It's just a bit airless in here, that's all. I'll have a walk–"

That slow burn deep inside crept up again as their eyes locked.

"Please let me take you out for lunch again, Lauren? You'd actually be doing me a favour. It's terribly dull staying with old relatives sometimes, and besides, it would atone for nearly knocking you over. How could you leave me with such a dreadful Karmic burden?"

The voice was not her own. It was as if a stranger stood beside her, and she heard herself say, "Okay. Yes, why not?"

His face broke into a delighted smile. "Really?"

She nodded and reached for her coat. Well, what harm would it do? It was something nice for a change. Not more than a few hours ago she'd craved this, longed for it! And besides, she was more than capable of putting a stop to the whole thing any time she liked.

"You're very lovely, you know?" he added. "Frankly, you've no idea how pretentious and shallow most people are that I come into contact with. And I've met the most incredibly beautiful women, but you – well, you're real, genuine, and that's such a rare and special quality."

She tried not to smart at the implication she wasn't in the same league looks-wise as the women he normally dated. "Thank you."

He remained seated, deep in thought, before suddenly brightening. "I know! Why don't I take you to Folly Point? Have you heard of it?"

She'd stood up and was fastening the new coat. "No, I haven't."

"Allegedly the best restaurant in the Marches."

She pictured a Michelin starred establishment with extortionately expensive haute cuisine. What happened to tea and cake? "Um–"

"My treat." He smiled into her eyes. "Actually, I've been looking for an excuse to go. And you said you wanted to know more about the castles around here. Well, this one was turned into the most amazing bistro. You'll love it."

She hesitated.

The moment spun around and around like dice on a roulette wheel.

The question came again - what harm would it do? It was a night out, one evening, a bit of fun sandwiched between all the trauma of the past four years with Sebastian and an uncertain future. A picture of Clingbine Cottage reared up at the same time, with its gap between the curtains, and the cranking bars of the electric fire as she sat in the dark, praying there'd be no more nightmares.

She nodded. "All right. Thank you, I'd love to."

He bounced out of his chair and grabbed his raincoat. "Excellent. And now I really must dash. I'm supposed to be the guest of honour tonight. Dullsville frankly, but hey-ho!"

About to leave, Wil suddenly paused, stepped back and kissed her lightly on the cheek. "I'm going to need your number."

She wrote it down.

He tucked it into his pocket. "Thursday?"

"Sure."

After he'd gone, she hung back a while. Her insides

were skittering, but tamping the feeling down she told herself nothing about this was wrong. A single man was taking a single woman out to dinner. And all they'd done was enjoy each other's company on one of the most wet and depressing afternoons of the year. A fresh belt of rain pelted the windows and she sighed at the thought of her faux fur being ruined. It might be best to put the old coat back on? Waiting until she heard the door click shut behind him, Lauren picked up her carrier and took it out. Crumpled, the coat was still damp with mud. It seemed such a shame to have to put it on again, but what choice was there?

With luck he'd be long gone and wouldn't see her as she scurried down the street to the pay and display. What an incongruous match, they were! What had she done accepting a date with him? Still, at least with staying at a place as grim as Clingbine Cottage there'd be no temptation to invite him in on Thursday evening. She almost laughed. This would be a one-off meal out, a tiny slice of fun. There was nothing to lose. And didn't he say they were having a family Halloween party at the house? Presumably after that he'd return to London and quickly forget her.

An evening out was all it was. One date. Nothing more.

And yet, and yet...what was the snag and tug of the hook deep inside, twisting and turning in the most tender part of her, the part where the nerves join the soul?

With the men in the bar still eyeing her openly, Lauren decided not to change into the muddy coat until she'd stepped into the outside porch. The rain was pelting down now, bouncing off the pavement, and there was no one in sight as she swapped coats and then sprinted down the

High Street clutching the carrier bag to her chest.

Most of the shop windows were now unlit, canopies dripping, and few cars passed. Had they really talked all afternoon? Squally rain blurred her vision as she tore down the cobbled alleyway to the car park, breathing a sigh of relief it was empty apart from her Mini. It wouldn't have looked great if he'd seen her looking like a drowned rat.

Oh, what does it matter?

She opened the car door and jumped in. It mattered. Her heart, whether she wanted it to or not, was skipping beats.

***

CHAPTER SIXTEEN

Late afternoon and dense fog had blanketed the moors. Braking to a crawl, Lauren squinted though the windscreen. In the reflected glare of the headlights, swathes of it rolled across the road, visibility down to a couple of yards. The engine sounded abnormally loud, and with the heater on full, suspended in an endless mass of grey cloud, it began to feel disorientating. Miles and miles of sodden turf lay on all sides, and ruminations on the lunchtime encounter were shelved as she gripped the wheel and scanned the road for the turn-off. Where the hell was Fiddlers Elbow? Had she passed it already?

I shouldn't have stayed so long. Stupid, stupid!

Then all of a sudden the sign to the pub flashed up ahead: a jaunty fiddler with one foot mid-tap, violin to his chin. What a sight for the weary traveller of old, she thought, picturing sweating horses clattering into the courtyard. A crystallised moment carried through time - of swaying lanterns, the sound of a faint tune coming from within, wood smoke heavy in the air. She was there… living it… could smell the wet straw in the stables, feel the sheets of cold rain. And was so captured by the vision she almost missed the junction.

At the last second she swung the wheel around, just as a corpse hanging from a noose lurched out of the fog. A partially decomposed face flew at the windscreen, and the body bounced heavily off the side of the bonnet. She yelped, her heart leapt, and the car snaked wildly on the bend.

"Holy crap! What the fuck was that?"

As the car veered alarmingly towards the boggy moorland she corrected the skid and only just managed to stay on the road. Well, Hannah had mentioned hangings but she hadn't expected to actually see them! The track had originally continued straight over at Fiddlers Elbow junction, disappearing across the moors towards Owlbury. A crossroads, then? And they used to hang people at crossroads, didn't they? She was gripping the steering wheel so tightly her knuckles gleamed white, eyes straining into a solid wall of fog for the turn-off to Groom Lake. It had been a ghost, that was all, just a ghost, the empty shell of Fiddlers Elbow already lost in the rear view mirror, swallowed whole.

This was really bad, she thought, slowly turning onto the lane. It was yellowish, like smog. She could end up driving across a field. The car could get stuck in a deep rut of mud. And then what?

"Shit! Why did I stay so long?"

You're very lovely, you know?

Why don't I take you to Folly Point?

Focusing intently on the road, an imaginary phone conversation insisted on playing out. He was going to phone, said he would. But they'd have to meet at the restaurant – she must drive herself there and back. What if she needed to leave? Or had to?

What would be the point of that? No, I'll pick you up. Then you can have a drink and relax.

I'd prefer to meet you there. Besides, I don't drink.

But Lauren, we're going to and from the same place.

No, honestly. I'd prefer...

The arch of trees closed overhead as the road dipped down towards Groom Lake, and the resemblance to a fairy tale landscape struck her anew, its familiar hush welcoming her home. The descent was steep, with the fog now more fragmented, floating across the lane in spectral wisps before drifting into the forest. And when the ford came into view at long last, she sighed with relief, slightly relaxing her tight grip on the wheel. That had been one hair-raising trip back!

The tyres swished through the flooded ford as she slowed and sought out the gateposts to the estate. He would have taken this exact route minutes ago, she was thinking, and was just about to swing the car into the drive when the headlights captured a startled face.

She had no time to react. The complexion was flour-white, eyes flashing from under a hood - a man, lean and agile, who quickly shot out of sight. Nor was he alone. In the shock of the moment she estimated around two or three others also darted out of the driveway, vanishing in an instant.

That was the man from the mill! Charon! What was he doing here?

Parking, she switched off the engine and sat perfectly still. The cottage stood in total darkness, the woods behind a mass of black. Those ducking out of sight with him had been a lot smaller; slight and quick. Children?

***

CHAPTER SEVENTEEN

The fog down in the valley was more of a dense drizzle. White wraiths glided across the drive and the occasional drop of water from overhanging branches plopped onto the roof. She checked the rear view mirror. Expecting to see what? A gang of hoodies hovering by the gates? But the lane was empty. They'd definitely gone.

Cautiously, Lauren inched open the car door.

The early evening air was damp and cold and she hurried to the cottage, key at the ready. An owl hooted from far away. What was Charon doing in the grounds? Poaching? Setting traps?

There's no life in these woods, so poaching for what?

It occurred to her that others may also have a key to this cottage, and once inside she dragged one of the kitchen chairs over and wedged it beneath the door handle. After checking her belongings were still there, she drew the curtains, turned on the fire, ramped up the heating, and then ran a steaming hot bath. All seemed okay but it was going to take a while to calm her nerves.

No one's been inside.

Was it Charon that first night? So what was he doing here?

And why was he with children?

Maybe it's all legit and they'd been up to the house?

It doesn't feel right…

Ten minutes later Lauren lay back in the bath. Everything since coming here had been downright disturbing. But today had been the oddest yet, starting with the paralysis at the lake. It was hard to remember all the details because she'd been in such a state of shock, the sequence and images now vague. One memory would forever remain imprinted on her mind, however - that of the voice. The deep, velvety, hypnotic voice and the sensation of falling onto downy pillows, looking through leaded windows at a night sky...
Déjà-vu. It skittered across her mind's eye with the soft, fluttering wings of an elusive butterfly. The voice! All she had to do was recall the words and instantly it was back in her head. *You loved it, Lauren. You wanted it. You always did...*
The voice, conjured too quickly, too easily.
Here her solar plexus lurched uncomfortably and again came the snag of a fish hook. It pulled at the tender spot located between the stomach and the heart, and for a second it felt like wobbling on a tightrope, knowing the safety net had gone. She put a flat palm to the skin, shutting out the voice, transferring all thoughts determinedly to what had happened this afternoon instead.
Wil. Wil who? Landgrave?
Who are you? Why did you pop into my life, and why now?
Maybe there was no need to be suspicious about every last thing? The encounter had been enjoyable, harmless, and just what she'd needed. Only this morning she'd complained about being lonely. Hadn't she yearned for arms around her? Maybe this was the universe giving her what she'd asked for? She deserved this, an interlude, some pleasure in what was a particularly difficult period in life. It was a good thing. Pleasurable. Nice. She soaped shampoo

into her hair. The way his gaze had flicked to her lips when he thought she wasn't looking, and the almost vulnerable, helpless softening of his features when they'd parted had not passed her by. But could a wealthy, well-connected man like him really be interested in someone like her?

I've met the most incredibly beautiful women…

Why not accept this was quite exciting and just enjoy it for however long it lasted? A tingle of exhilaration fizzed inside. For several moments she relived the way he'd stood behind her at the bar, the scent of him – leather, citrus, sandalwood and rain – re-conjuring the anticipation. The emotions were intensely reminiscent of times gone by, of first loves, innocent yet laced with danger… When without warning the scene catapulted in a quantum leap forwards to the two of them pushing into each other, her back rammed against a stone wall, his narrow hips pulsing into hers, demanding hands pushing her sweater up…

Suddenly the water was far too hot. She yanked out the plug, speedily towelled off, and grabbed her dressing gown. This was foolish in the extreme. She'd known him for only a few hours. For goodness sake! She wasn't like this. Had never been like this. Not since a few regretful encounters as a teen, anyway - ones Sebastian had coaxed out of her and then thrown back in her face. Shame burned her cheeks.

After making camomile tea, Lauren sat by the fire listening to the silence. What had she done, spending all that money on a silly coat and a cheap, trashy bag? And now her head was full of sex when her predicament was so dire, and there were urgent needs that should be focused on. He'd regressed her twenty years.

Since this morning… All since this morning…

The tea calmed her. Was there a reason for meeting him?

Were these things destined? Or was she being drawn into the strange dark magic of the lake? Her mind did not feel her own, the voice inside oscillating between reason and insanity. Why was her head so woolly? Why couldn't she think clearly?

There'd also been the vivid dream of an underground chamber with cobbled floors; a dismal funereal ceremony, and the man who'd done something terrible, something that tortured his soul.

What else had happened? Oh, yes - Hannah. Hannah, who was a healer. Hannah who'd told her about the hangings and been unable to even walk around here because of the effect on her. Surely, to have met her after all these years could not be coincidence? Especially in such an insular area with so few incomers. What were the odds?

And then so many ghosts: from the old man with a stick on the lane, to the rising spectres in the woods, and the corpse swinging from a noose at Fiddlers Elbow.

Putting her fingers together she bent her head and prayed. She hadn't prayed for years. Yet here in this place fear had seeped through the cracks of normality, an icy chill breezing deep into her psyche.

Never had she felt fear of the unseen, of what may lie beyond the veil of daily life. But now dread blew all around on an ill wind. It rattled at the door and tapped on the windows, scratched at the walls and haunted her dreams. She pressed her hand firmly against the tender part she instinctively felt was her soul, to where the nerves were tightly bound.

"Please, God. Please send me direction. Help me see what to do, where to go..."

A stream of questions came without answers. Why had life

led her here? And who was this man, Wil? She knew almost nothing about him, while she'd told him just about everything about herself. Gradually her thoughts wandered out of prayer and into deciding what to do if he phoned.
She'd said yes.
But he'd yet to confirm.
He Will!
But should she go?
Already in her mind she was falling against him again, the caress of his hand on her back as her body pressed into his; safe and warm, wanted and loved.
"My weakness?"
After all, it really had been a very, very long time.
All was quiet and still around the cottage, broken only by the occasional flurry of leaves at the door and the drip of a roof leak. Fatigue was pulling her down and she jerked awake. What would happen if she dreamed again? She must try to stay awake as long as possible. Another long night lay ahead though, and there really was no option, especially after drinking that afternoon. Her head lolled and she forced herself to switch off the fire, make up a hot water bottle and go to bed. With luck it would be a deep and dreamless sleep? God only knew she was tired enough. 'Keep thinking of Wil,' she told herself. 'Think of good things, exciting things, and don't think about the lake. Don't think about what happened!'
And when she closed her eyes, it was to picture him across the table at the old black and white inn, recalling with ease how his gaze had rarely left hers, and how confidant his voice was – sonorous and richly resonant, each syllable the strum of a bass guitar string. God, the voice, the voice…The heat from the hot water bottle was permeating

her back, as enveloped in the warm cocoon of the sleeping bag, she had no further conscious thoughts before falling seamlessly into the dark embrace of oblivion.

When consciousness flickered again, however, the room was still coal face black. *Not morning*! But something was wrong, had woken her. Half asleep, she tried to rid herself of what felt like a cough, a pressure on her chest. But it grew heavier and she coughed again, rolling onto her back. There was a weight compressing her lungs, getting worse, and soon she found she was struggling for breath.

Wake up! Lauren, wake up!

On a deep subconscious level she was aware of trying to respond to the command, but could not; and of trying to draw breath, but was unable to. Panic slammed in. Something, no, someone, was sitting on top of her chest! And exactly as had happened at the lake, she was paralysed, the breath in her lungs iron-rigid. She could not breathe in or out. As the weight on top of her, which she slowly began to realise was pulsating, now took form.

"Hello, Lauren!"

She opened her eyes. Ah, a dream. It was only a dream. And a good one. Nice…The man was Sebastian. How she loved him. How desperately the whole of her wanted to merge with him, to fuse, to be transported and carried into bliss. He was lowering himself onto her, the very first time they'd made love about to be re-lived - the way his eyes drank in her body, how he dipped his head to kiss her forehead, then her lips, then her throat…further and further down… Pleasure rippled through her, despite the lungs that were rigid and beginning to hurt.

"You are the most desirable woman I have ever, ever met…I can't get enough of you, Lauren. I can't believe how bloody, bloody lucky I am."

I'm dreaming. It's a memory.

I can't breathe.

And yet her body was responding of its own accord. Her back was arching, her insides melting to receive...But something wasn't quite right with the dream. There were claws digging into the soft flesh of her upper arms, and she was freezing. There was a bad smell, too – rotting, bad drains - like the one at the lake!

Her eyes snapped open. This wasn't Sebastian. This wasn't even a dream.

Sitting on top of her was a blacker than tar, gargoyle-ugly, demonic looking creature.

Wake up, Lauren! Wake up! Wake the fuck up!

Her lungs had become an iron cage and her heart rate speeded up to an express train at full pelt. The thing on top of her was now slowly turning around, showing her what it was about to stick inside her.

This is not real. It is not real. Wake up!

Prayer came from the subconscious, repeated in her mind, 'Our father, who art in heaven. Hallowed be thy name...Thy kingdom come...Thy will be done...'

Laughter ricocheted around the walls. 'You don't believe all that. You have no faith at all so it won't work. Your true self wants to come to me. You like this. You always did.'

She couldn't scream. No sound came out of her throat.

When suddenly there was a crash against the window. Glass shattered. Followed by another crash in the kitchen. And then the car alarm went off.

***

CHAPTER EIGHTEEN

Five in the morning and still dark outside.

Numb, Lauren sat in the kitchen. She imagined them running away up the lane, the same hooded figures seen sneaking out of the drive last night, boots splashing through the gushing water, no torches. Obviously they wanted her out of here.

She was fully dressed with all the heating and the lights on, a cup of hot camomile in front of her. Her hands were shaking as she picked up the mug, teeth chattering. What had been worse - the demonic nightmare or the physical attack?

It's time to leave. No more excuses, I have to go.

Unshed tears stung her eyes. All she had in the bank was enough for a modest down payment on a rented flat. One month. If only she hadn't thrown in her career to help Sebastian with his business. What a terribly vulnerable position to be in! She'd trusted him with everything she had. And now here she was on the brink of homelessness. All she'd wanted was a fortnight of respite to think out the next move, to not make any more mistakes. The irony being that even that had been a mistake.

Fortunately the windows hadn't broken, but both the kitchen and bedroom panes were shattered cobwebs that could easily give way. Ditto the car windscreen. Not only that but the mobile phone had no signal and there wasn't a land line. What to do?

Why the hell was her mind so foggy? The top of her head banged and every day was like wading through treacle.

She forced herself not to relive the nightmare, to consider nothing else but practicalities. Okay, first light - go up to the farm and tell the Moodys what had happened. Next, the car windscreen repair. Surely Tyler would help her out? Did he have a heart? That was the dilemma. Or did he feel like Charon and want her out of here? Why? What harm did she do?

They looked so like each other, him and Charon…

She stared into the bars of the fire. It was definitely Charon and whoever was living at the mill, children by the look of it, creeping round here at night. That it was them who'd smashed her windows was obvious. And Tyler had tried to scare her away from exploring the grounds. But it was hardly Tyler or Charon spooking the woods or infesting her dreams, was it? That was something they definitely couldn't do. In vain she tried to block the images of the horrific creature that had weighted down her lungs and mocked her for praying.

Hello, Lauren!

She shuddered. The voice had been the same as at the lake, along with the invasive worming into the deepest tunnels of her shame, fear and guilt. The night terror was connected, she was sure. All of it was connected.

Clasping the cup, she sipped the hot liquid, soothing herself. In some invisible way, spiritually, psychologically, she was being violated.

It seemed a long time before the first faint ray of light heralded what was a wintry dawn. And at seven she peered through the gap in the curtains. Thank God the night was over. At least no one had returned to break in or force the front door. And, she acknowledged, they could have done.

At what time was it reasonable to go up to the farm? The cottage wasn't secure now either, so she had the idea of putting her belongings in the car boot before driving up to the Moodys, praying the windscreen held out. The shattered screen was only on the passenger side at the moment, and they'd be bound to know of a local garage.

By eight she had the boot packed with her bags, the items just bought, and a carrier of food stuff. Those at the mill could break in here with one tap of a hammer on weakened glass, scavenge like hyenas and be off without a trace. Obviously they were living on the edge, but if they were truly criminal then well, wasn't it a bit risky to be living so close to a high court judge? Maybe she could go up to the house and tell them what had happened? Tell Wil?

Or would that risk repercussions? How violent was Charon?

She bit her lip, struck by indecision. Police? Maybe the Moodys first? See what they said? One step at a time, anyway.

Locking the boot, she walked back inside. A piece of toast still lay where she'd left it twenty minutes before and she forced it down. Tiredness was burning her eyes as she dusted off her old jacket and headed for the door.

"Well, goodbye Clingbine Cottage, I can't say I'll miss you!"

A layer of fog hovered over the open fields as she drove out of the wooded valley. Where could she stay, though? If only she hadn't bought that stupid coat.

"No, this whole thing has been disastrous. I need to get a job. And I have to get the car sorted today - priority."

What if Glynis offered a rebate?

"I mean, it's unreasonable to expect anyone to stay there now. I'm entitled to a rebate. And that would pay for a week at a B&B and buy time to find a flat and a job. Sounds like a plan. Yes, that would really, seriously help… Well, if Glynis is amenable, that is... But how can she not be?"

As she drove, talking to an imaginary Glynis, the malevolent incubus flew back into her mind, the stink of it, and the mockery reverberating around her head as she'd prayed.

You have no faith at all so it won't work. Your true self wants to come to me. You like this…You always did…

Always did? Hadn't the voice at the lake said something similar? What was it now?

A crippling idea rode in, that the demon had jumped into her head yesterday morning, and this was possession and she would change character, become deranged, be drugged and locked up. Even thinking about the vile creature seemed to re-conjure its existence, and soon every detail began to expand until the shame of her own body's response replayed once more.

You loved it, Lauren. You wanted it. You always did!

"No! Get out of my head. Get out of my head!"

She was shouting out loud, and realised as the farmhouse loomed ahead, just how insane she must look.

Tyler Moody was setting down a dish for the chained dog in the yard, when he turned at the sound of her car. As she got out and began to explain why she was there, however, his face told her what she needed to know - the attack on the cottage was news to him. Relief washed through her.

"It was about three this morning. Stones were thrown at the bedroom window and then the kitchen. They're not broken but they're fractured, and as you can see my car was hit as well."

He stared at her.

"And when I came back from Owlbury yesterday I saw a man in a hoodie lurking around the gates. He had some kids with him but they all vanished as soon as they saw the car. I didn't see who did this, obviously - I was fast asleep. It's just, well, it could be they were the poachers you were telling me about? Maybe they don't like me being here?"

It's Charon and you know it.

He shrugged and pulled a face, then went back inside and shouted upstairs. "Glynis! You're wanted. Get your arse down here."

A string of expletives came shrieking back.

Lauren hugged herself. Drizzle was blowing across the fields in a cross wind, and she stamped her feet to keep warm.

Re-emerging, Tyler gestured to the car. "You'll have to get that fixed."

"I know. Do you have the number of a local garage?"

He nodded. "On the mobile. I'll go and get it."

"Thanks."

While she waited, Lauren went over to the collie and bent down. "Don't worry, I won't touch you. You're lovely, that's all, and I wish you were mine. I could do with a guard dog, especially a beautiful one like you."

He whimpered softly as she held out a hand for him to nuzzle.

"Right," said Glynis, who'd come out of the house wearing an anorak over her pyjamas. "What's happened, then?"

Straightening up, Lauren related what she'd told Tyler, hoping she'd gauged the situation correctly - that Glynis had gone against her husband's wishes in order to make a bit of cash for herself, that Tyler knew Charon was responsible, both men wanted her gone, and none of them wanted the police out here. Just a guess. So Glynis was on her own and in a fix if she didn't offer a rebate?

"I think I'll report it to the police, as well."

"Oh no, you don't want to do that."

"Why not?"

"No one's going to come out here, is it? It'll just be those kids. Nothing they can do."

"But it's on the judge's estate, so maybe Lord Landgrave will want them to do something? I've got to be honest, I know I've paid you for two weeks but I don't feel safe there now. I think I'd prefer a rebate."

"No, no rebate."

Lauren's heart rate began to speed up and heat swept into her face. "Well, it's not safe there and I can't just leave without a rebate, that wouldn't be fair. But if you won't reimburse me I'll have to call the police and get the property made safe. You wouldn't want to stay there on your own, would you?"

Glynis frowned.

"So which is it to be?"

"Look, I'll have the windows fixed today, all right? They'll be done today so it'll be the same as it was before, isn't it?"

Lauren regarded her steadily.

That money's long gone. She's in such a crock of shit with Tyler and Charon.

Glynis's stare was hard as nails.

She definitely wasn't budging and Lauren's nerves took a fresh hit. No way was Glynis going to reimburse her: the woman's jaw was jutting. Man, what kind of trouble was she in?

"To be honest, I think the police should be called and I ought to have a rebate. It's not fit to live in and I'm badly shaken as I'm sure you can imagine. Goodness knows who these thugs are."

Except I know who did this and so do you.

"No. No need for that. Just kids, I told you. We'll have the windows fixed today." She indicated the car. "And Ty will tell you where to go to get that done. We'll ring now. It's his cousin, see?"

The thought of having to tolerate a few more nights at the cottage filled her with dismay. But Glynis had her arms folded and the glare was pure granite.

"All right then," said Lauren. "As long as they're all fixed and secured today." She'd have to get a rental sorted online. Straight away. As soon as.

Glynis rubbed her arms as a cold breeze whipped off the mountains and blasted them both in a swirl of icy leaves. "Nasty business, anyhow."

"Yes." *Thanks for caring.*

"What time did it happen?"

"About three this morning."

"Anything taken?"

"No. It looks like they just wanted to scare me."

Glynis narrowed her eyes. "Little shits."

"Which kids did you mean, by the way? You said it was

just kids."

Glynis glanced over her shoulder as Tyler emerged from the house. "Oh, I dunno, is it? Just them up at the house, I expect. I told you–"

"This is where you take the car," he said, handing Lauren a business card. "And you'll be wanting a rebate, I expect? Maybe go and stay in a nice hotel instead?"

A dark cloud landed on Glynis. "No rebate," she snapped. "The windows will be done by five. Our Neil will do it. I've told her. All settled. Anyhow, I'm going inside now. Bloody freezing, I am."

Lauren tapped the card. "Thanks for this. I'll go straight there."

He was still standing in the driveway, watching, as she reversed out of the yard and set off down the lane. But it wasn't until she'd reached the top of the long track out of Groom Lake and turned left towards Fiddlers Elbow, that Lauren looked back. From across the valley, Woodsay Castle could just be seen over the top of the tree line.

On impulse she pulled over. A beam of pale light seemed to point directly at the ruins, transforming them into a glimmering illusion of medieval splendour. The poignant beauty pierced her heart and in that instant it was as if she'd swum up to the surface of a deep and murky pond, shaken the filthy water from her hair and glimpsed the brilliance of the sun.

"I can't leave, can I? It feels as though this was all somehow meant to be. But why? Why has fate brought me here?"

This darkness had done its best to infest her mind: it had attacked her with her own weakness, replacing love with a cheap trick. It had tried to invade her soul and her body with a diabolical incubus, and now it had caused her to be physically threatened.

Was it destiny, a lesson to be learned? Or was it an unlucky run-in with evil - pure chance that scored a bulls-eye with someone who had no idea it even existed?

"Well then", she murmured, starting up the engine. "Maybe now I see you, I can arm myself a bit better."

Thinking about Hannah and wondering what she knew about the spiritual, about the merging of timelines and dark magic, she tied a scarf around her face in case the windscreen shattered further, and pulled back onto the road. Should she get in touch with Hannah?

They were hiding something here. That was the feeling. Something Glynis possibly didn't fully know about or understand, but Tyler and Charon most certainly did. And likely it concerned the young girl in the woods, the clandestine figures at the mill, and the malignant power of the lake.

Turning right at Fiddlers Elbow towards Owlbury, the question bugged her. Perhaps none of what had happened to her was coincidence? Maybe she was here for a reason, and maybe, just maybe, she wasn't supposed to run away from her demons this time, but face them? And there was something else, too. There was no doubt she was being attacked by dark forces, things unseen and even unacknowledged by most people, which made it all the more isolating. But there was also no doubt she was being protected… *Get out now! Wake up, Lauren!*

"Thank you," she said aloud. "I can't see you but I hear you… Thank you."

***

CHAPTER NINETEEN

By the time Lauren returned to Clingbine Cottage it had gone lunchtime. Parking the Mini, she grabbed a carrier bag from the boot and hurried inside. The morning had been productive, though. While waiting for the windscreen to be fixed, she'd made full use of the garage's Wi-Fi to search for a job and somewhere to live. Maybe she'd go back home? If you could call it home just because you grew up there? The whole thing had taken hours, but at least the car was now driveable.

After lunch she sat at the kitchen table by the wall. On that first night when she'd had to get up and sit by the fire because of the cold, a memory had stirred. It had been of a childhood holiday that made no sense, and now it flashed fleetingly into her mind again - a damp cottage and the flicker of a long track with green fields either side. But this time it was accompanied by a vague smell of musty clothes and the sound of rain pummelling the roof. That couldn't be, though. It just couldn't. Auntie Claire had taken her away only once and that had been to the Gower Peninsula. They'd talked about it often, with Claire saying how she regretted not being able to afford to take her away again, that it had just been the once.

She shook her head. It was a weird déjà-vu thing again, this place playing with her sanity.

Think of something else, something practical...

So would they come to fix the windows? When? Was she to sit here all afternoon? Frankly, even the prospect of one more night was daunting and it could be days yet. What if no one turned up and Glynis had fobbed her off? How about just a cut and run – get out of here now and never look back?

Had she not run away all her life, though - escaping one unhappy situation only to jump into another? And some indefinable thing held her here. This one seemed to go so much deeper, the psychic attacks uncannily personal. Why? Her dreams were infested in such an intimate and all-knowing way. It was almost as if the boundaries between herself and Groom Lake were porous, and an ancient drama was pulling her through an invisible curtain onto another stage. To be trapped forever?

But it's not just me!

Others had also remarked on the strangeness here - almost everyone she'd met, in fact. History seemed to bleed into the present day. How could that happen?

The man who disappeared was sent mad by what he saw. Jumped to his death is most likely. Wouldn't be the first time round here!

She made another coffee. But the answers to all her questions remained elusive. Maybe start with the personal bit, and the fears she constantly tamped down? After all, that was the only part she had a hope of controlling. Why was she forever running away? Did a hideous fear lie deep inside? Because if that was the case, then no matter where she ran there'd be no escape. And that thing, the voice, whatever it was that had tapped into her weaknesses, had both extracted and magnified each and every one of them.

It knew every last detail, forcing a re-enactment.

Face it!

Face what, though? Was there something to face?

Half way through the second coffee she put the cup down and looked at her watch. The thought of sitting here until either Neil, the window-repairer, turned up, or it went dark, was insufferable. She had to get out, even if only for an hour. Maybe go for a walk and get a better look at D'Avranches Grange? Why, she could not say, only that the compulsion to view it again was a strong one.

'What about from the hill,' she thought, already grabbing her walking boots. 'A bird's eye view?'

Outside, however, she hesitated. Which route to take? She eyed the tall grey pines. Taking the short cut over to the Moodys' drive would be a hell of a lot quicker, but meant skirting those woods. The periphery path was nowhere near the lake though, and didn't involve going into the forest at all. Five minutes or less and she'd be over the stile and straight onto the track to the hill. Back pretty soon – a couple of hours? The windows might be done by then.

Still she wavered, inclined to take the lane and the long way round. No, it would be okay. The path ran adjacent to the back of the cottage garden just behind the netting. She could see it from here. It was crazy to go all the way up the road. So with only a brief backwards glance at the car, double checking it was locked and trying not to worry, she made a supreme effort to switch to positive thoughts and set off. All would be well. It would. Yes, it would definitely be okay. There was a reason she was here, and now she acknowledged that possibility there was a feeling she'd known it all along. All she had to do was find out why.

As well as seeking out jobs and flats in her native town that morning, she'd also researched the Landgrave family. There hadn't been much information other than official titles and long lists of achievements and accolades. Nothing personal had surfaced, however. There were no interviews or photographs of note, save one official black and white avatar of the judge. She'd studied him closely. Although the picture was only of his face, he seemed angular and bony, and she imagined he was tall, possibly stooped. Bald with almost no chin, his eyes were dark and intense as he stared into the camera, and by far his most distinguishable feature. It was the shape of them – like inverted semi-circles or segments of an orange. His wife, Dolly, was barely mentioned and there were no children. Was he in residence now? Must be if Wil was staying with them? Was he Wil's blood uncle or was the family connection through Dolly? There wasn't much of a resemblance. Actually there wasn't one at all.

Wil! The prospect of tomorrow night's date suddenly bounced back into her thoughts like a cuckoo bursting out of a clock. She'd almost forgotten. How could she possibly go? And what about paying half? Her stomach plunged. *Oh, God!* But on the other hand, to take the gift of another meal would mean being indebted.

She looked up at the sky. Already a fine net of mist was descending. And the instant she stepped into the woods the temperature plummeted. There was nothing to worry about, she told herself, nothing at all. Not abnormal - just the cool of the forest. Nowhere near the lake. Not going into the middle so it was perfectly all right. Five minutes tops.

"Got to stand up to my fears anyway," she muttered. "I

will not run and I will not be afraid. Ghosts can't hurt me."

The pines were a regiment of tall sentinels; the only sound her footsteps and quick short breaths. Nothing here felt alive. It was as if winter's chill never left. Even the ivy had fallen from its climb, hanging in tendrils or dying half way up. The place was so unnaturally still and watchful. Yes, watchful… A shiver traced up and down her spine and the fine nerves on her skin began to prickle. The afternoon was darkening…

Just my imagination.

Yep, just her imagination. And she kept telling herself that even as a shadow formed overhead, stretching along the path in front faster than she could walk.

No sun. The day was gloomy. No sun meant no shadows.

There was an uptick in her heart rate. She picked up pace almost to a jog. "Not afraid, not afraid, not afraid..."

But it happened fast.

Like a crowd rushing through a door, what had been silent was suddenly alive with hissing gossip and shifting shades. Except, unlike before, this was way too quick, and in the single moment it took to register what was happening it was already too late. The ground dragged at the soles of her boots, and her legs were instantly weighted with iron. The nightmare of running but not moving, of being stuck on an eternal loop, of never getting out, never getting home, had her in its grip inside of a second.

Shocked, she found that once again she could hardly move. Why the paralysis? Every time? My God, she was only on the very edge of the woods! The stile at the far end of the path was tantalisingly close though, and she forced herself towards it, the shimmering mirage of emerald fields behind vivid and surreal. Each step was painfully slow and heavy, the thump of each heartbeat leaden, solid, and… final?

As the vison of green waxed and waned before her, the desire to slump to the path and give up became overwhelming. She fought to keep her eyes open. A myriad of tree trunks swirled all around and she stumbled dizzily, drunkenly, until forced to stop. It felt like a heart attack, a banging ache in the chest, each thudding pulse in her left arm and neck an iron squeeze. Bending double, she gasped for each laboured breath, hands on her knees, slowly counting from one to ten. It was a trick, not real, she was fit and well… Until slowly, oh-so-gradually, it became apparent that something had changed.

She looked up sharply.

Firstly, the whispering had stopped. The woods were absolutely silent, the air one of anticipation, on pause. And secondly, when had it turned black as night?

Her pounding heart was now calming, the stile ahead shining as magically as a stag in a sunlit glade.

How seamlessly she'd accepted this, she thought – the reality of spiritual warfare, dark versus light.

"I see you and I know what you're doing," she said quietly. "Come on, Lauren. A thirty second push!"

Each step was like wading fully dressed into an oncoming tide, but with grim determination she gained ground, and no sooner had she grabbed the stile and hauled herself up the wooden steps, than all the heaviness drained away, so rapidly she almost flew over the top. The ground reared up and she landed with a crack.

Bloody hell! It would be madness to ever go in there again. Not ever. So it wasn't just the lake, then? The magnetic force held the whole area, so powerful it even expanded into dreams.

It took a while to recover, despite the episode lasting probably less than a minute; but acutely aware now of the drizzle on her hair and skin, she glanced up at the path leading to the castle. The stones glistened, the ruins at the top floating in and out of clouds.

"I'm not going mad. I will not be jumping off the cliff. And I will not be put off."

What was she to do? Run back down to the road quaking in fear, and flee? She'd always had nightmares, had always reacted out of nervous fear, clinging to anyone who would take it from her, if only for the shortest time. This had to be faced, the whole thing, no matter how bad it got. Besides, there wasn't anyone to cling to anymore.

She hauled herself up.

"Okay, what am I looking for? There's something that will make sense of this. Maybe I've got a few days, maybe only now, but there's something."

Busy thoughts came and went as she climbed, deliberately not revisiting what had just happened. The more she thought about the lake, the child, the voice, and the underground ceremony, the more real it became, the more insistent and invasive.

Switching her mind to more earthly matters she began to wonder what to do about Wil and what to say when he rang? *If* he rang. Maybe he wouldn't? No, but what if he did? What excuse? And how come she'd agreed anyway? It wasn't as if she could pretend to be in any way normal: a woman simply having a holiday, reading and walking, before going home to a job, family and friends. She had no family, and very few friends. No one to call on. No one to wonder what had happened to her should she go missing.

Shut up, shut up, shut up!

And why was Wil even interested in her - a man with obvious enormous wealth? Why had he not brought an international model or actress here for the party? Why was he here alone? In fact, had yesterday been a coincidence at all, now she came to think about it?

Shut up, Lauren!

Frowning, she continued the climb, and was up to the first level of the hill when a plaintive wail broke into her mind chatter. Carried downwind, it whined through the castle walls, trailing into the mist, and still panting from the exertion she took the cue to stop and get her breath. The edge was a matter of yards away. Could be she didn't need to go any higher and the house could be seen from here?

She wandered over and crouched low.

Groom Lake Woods flanked the Grange to the north. But the house itself, well hidden from all angles of approach below, was clearly visible from above. Every bit of its layout. Instinctively she dropped down. Few people would ever come here because the path wasn't signposted, and there was nowhere to park on the road below. And even if they did, they'd probably do what she'd also done on the first day and climb straight to the top – to the castle and the view of the mountains. Not only that, but the house would be out of eyeshot further up. This, it seemed, was the only spot.

The drizzly fog cleared sporadically, revealing an empty courtyard. D'Avranches Grange was far more substantial than it appeared from the lake, with two wings overlooking what was actually a magnificent courtyard at the back. The windows were long and leaded with pointed arches, and the upper floors had French doors opening onto balconies. The front of the house, with its tree- lined sweeping driveway, had a large gravel turning area which also led through an archway to the courtyard. But it was what had been built behind the house, beyond the old stables, in a densely wooded copse, that took the breath.

"Wow!"

A temple? A Roman temple? Pearlescent white, complete with columns and a set of steps up to a grand entrance, it was completely incongruous with the Welsh Marchlands. How extraordinary! What on earth did they use it for? Maybe it was instead of the usual estate church? A different religion? But why hide such a stunning building? No one would know it was there unless they were guests at the house or standing at this vantage point.

The image seared onto her mind's eye. She'd been meant to see it today, hadn't she? The compulsion had been so strong. And the impact of that was just beginning to register, when all further thoughts were shelved due to the whir of an incoming text message. She scrabbled for the phone. It was him. He was confirming.

Fleetingly, just before picking it up, she saw herself hovering between two worlds, the moment somehow pivotal.

'Hi Lauren! Booked Folly Point tomorrow night at 8pm. I'll pick you up. Wil.'

No! No, he wouldn't. Why the hell had she agreed to this?

Yet at the same time, her heart was dancing.

She stared at the neon text. Oh God, she was going to go, wasn't she?

Well, he couldn't pick her up. On that point she'd

definitely make a stand. Independence was crucial. But where was Folly Point? Actually, it might be easier if he drove. Damn, what to do? She bit her lip. Another sheet of rain was moving in, and the walk back would have to be the long way via the lane, a good hour.

Maybe ensure the windows were fixed before replying? Then again there was no phone signal at the cottage.

Her finger hovered over the phone.

Reply now?

Rain began to spot.

No, I'll set back, think while I walk.

Though already she knew - no matter what the situation with the windows or awkwardness over the bill, she'd definitely be having dinner with this man. Somewhere in the book of fate, it was written.

***

Chapter Twenty

Folly Point was a fairy-tale castle, Gothic and quirky by design. Allegedly built as a rich man's folly – something to please the eye - the turreted tower stood on the pinnacle of a wooded hill, yet only came into view at the last moment, after taking the final bend on a long narrow drive that spiralled steeply to the top.

Lauren gasped as she drove under the ivy-covered archway. On the west side of the tower there was a walled al-fresco area. Potted palms and low lights immediately conjured an air of summer enchantment, although tonight the cobbles gleamed wetly, and the tables and chairs were deserted. She headed towards the carpark at the back. Having just navigated the helter-skelter drive with no passing-places, she made a mental note not to let a single drop of alcohol pass her lips: the thought of meeting another car on the way down was hair raising enough.

In the quiet of the car she checked her reflection.

Was this the right decision? Tamping down a splutter of nerves, she looked into her own eyes. It just felt... What? As if everything since coming here had led to this?

He knew he was going to bring me here. Tea and cake, my arse! What am I doing here? Really? I could go and never look back.

Then again, what if she had the time of her life? What

if it was brilliant? Was she always going to run scared? She'd run the gauntlet of the haunted woods, hadn't she? Well then, she could do dinner with a handsome man. Because that, she told herself, was all this was. Just a dinner date.

Glynis had been waiting in the truck when she'd returned sopping wet from the walk yesterday. The windows had, as promised, been repaired, and a bolt and chain had even been put on the door for added peace of mind.

"I saw your car so I knew you couldn't be far away," she'd said, looking Lauren up and down. "You must be a keen walker, isn't it?"

"I got caught out, that's all."

"You'll catch your death."

"Don't worry, I'll be fine. I'm pleased you got the windows fixed, anyway. Although I'm still not sure I want to spend another night here."

The two women stood in the drive, both eager to get out of the rain.

"It's only kids, I told you. They definitely won't give you any more trouble."

"Even so, I might have a word with the Landgraves," Lauren said.

"No need. We've told them about it. And besides, me and Ty are responsible for the cottage."

"Have you? Told the Landgraves about it?"

There was a second's hesitation before Glynis replied. "Yes, so you've no need to worry. They're as upset about it as we are. I'm sure you can imagine."

"Yes."

Last night had passed, however, without further

incident and she'd slept soundly. And so here she was, in her little black dress and new coat, clutching the shiny, patent bag.

Okay then, here goes!

Inside the tower an inglenook fireplace spanning most of one wall, crackled with logs, the smoky air laced with garlic and wine. A little uncertain, she stood in the stone-walled entrance to what was an open dining room with no visible reception or bar. It was like walking straight into a private party, she was thinking, as the arched oak door behind clunked firmly shut. A flush shot up to her face. What to do? Walk in or hope a waiter appeared? She looked at her watch. Ten minutes late. Where was Wil?

The low murmur of congenial conversation was occasionally punctuated by bursts of laughter, the overall impression being one of subdued but immense wealth – oak panelling, white-clothed tables glinting with crystal, and a family crest above the fireplace.

One or two heads turned her way and just as it was becoming awkward and she was contemplating making a swift exit, Wil appeared, so stealthily it caused her to step back, startled. That was the second time he'd done that, she realised, trying not to let astonishment show on her face. And he looked...different... Was it the low light? But the contrast between the black of his hair and the white of his shirt seemed far more pronounced than it had before - dazzling, in fact, a shock to the senses. His presence totally negated the rest of the room and she struggled to adjust.

There was an international feeling about Wil, she thought, as the now familiar scent of sandalwood, leather, citrus, and something indefinable, salty, lingered between them. He would look as at home in Klosters as he would in a London club or on a country estate.

He had hold of both her hands. "You look gorgeous."

"Thank you."

"Come on over to the table. I've ordered champagne."

Her voice sounded shrill and overly loud as she followed him through the restaurant. Did she have an accent? Was she speaking properly? There hadn't been a single pause in conversation when she'd entered, but now it had fallen to a hush as he sped away, and she found herself inadvertently replying to his back.

"Oh no, I'm sorry but I can't drink. I'm sorry but I have to..."

The Maître D' pulled back a chair for her.

"Um, thank you."

"Your coat, Madam?"

Wil sat down as she shrugged off her coat, already instructing the man, "You can bring it now."

"Wil–"

He'd turned to beckon someone.

"Wil! Please–"

"I hope you notice we have a lovely table by the fire again?"

"Yes, thank you. But I have to tell you I can't drink. I've to drive back and the lane up here is–"

"We'll both get a taxi."

"Out here?"

"Of course."

Mindful that one or two people had glanced over, she lowered her voice.

"Actually, I really don't drink–"

"Lauren, you knocked back two ciders at lunch the other day. Strong ones, too."

She frowned. Strong ones? "I know, but this is champagne."

The bottle was brought to their table in a bucket of ice. "Sir. Madam. Taittinger, Comtes de Champagne, Grand Cru."

Wil nodded, the cork was duly extracted with a subtle 'thwop,' and sparkling, golden liquid poured into two crystal flutes.

All she saw was the ease of his smile. He wanted to please her that was all. Where were her manners?

"Okay, thank you. Just a little, though. With the meal."

After the waiter replaced the bottle into the ice, Wil raised his glass. "Well, here's to an enormously pleasant evening. I can't tell you how much I've been looking forward to this."

The first dish was local freshwater trout with caviar and a coconut and lemongrass velouté. Each course, of which there were six, merited a different wine, and all were interspersed with a variety of palette cleansers. It was difficult to decide which one was the most delicious, she thought, tasting the most sublime sauces, exquisite seafood and aromatic wines imaginable. And the culinary delights were surpassed only by the warm ambience of the room and the most intriguing company.

As she began to relax she became increasingly aware of the somewhat unusual fellow diners. Black tie didn't really describe the dress code. A couple of the men wore pointed red shoes. Some of the women wore floor length, backless gowns, and others had on the kind of bizarre designs usually confined to the fashion crowd. An older lady, she noticed with one quick glance, was wearing a harlequin jumpsuit and purple boots with bells on. Their eyes met and Lauren immediately returned her attention to Wil.

He was just putting down his glass. "That is so good," he said. "An exceptional Cotes du Rhone Chablis, don't you think? Now, where was I?"

She'd phased out for only a few seconds, momentarily distracted by the fellow guests and the odd artefacts in the display cabinets, which were now blurring with the walls - skulls? Miniature skulls? Far more talkative than last time, Wil had a huge repartee of anecdotes and it was non-stop. In fact he was quite the raconteur, with such a skilful talent for mimicry that he seemed to actually become the person he imitated. It was uncanny, and she found herself astounded, at times laughing until tears streamed down her face. The man was good. A couple of glasses of wine, though, and he was a chameleon. Not to mention incredibly good looking. Did she dare to dream?

When he paused to eat, she tuned into the background hum, realising most of the languages being spoken were not actually English or Welsh, but a mixture of European and what sounded like Romanian or perhaps Czech.

"Lichtenstein," said Wil.

"Sorry?"

"That's Count and Countess Borga. The one in the clown outfit's from Vienna. And then you have Susan and Kristoff – they're from Monte Carlo, friends of the Grimaldis."

"Really?"

"They come from all over the world to dine here by the way, not just Europe. How's the monkfish?"

She nodded. "Oh, gorgeous. It's lovely with pak choi, and wasabi."

He indicated her full glass. "You need to drink that

because I've ordered something a bit special for you to try next. It will be incredibly interesting to see if you can tell what it is."

She drained the Gewurztraminer and nodded. "Wow, that's heady - aromatic and kind of oily."

"Wonderful with spicy dishes, isn't it?" He twisted round at the approach of the waiter. "Ah, here we go."

"Now, Lauren I want you to tell me what you think this is."

Two plates were set in front of them, and she found herself looking at several pale-coloured chunks of something coated in a greyish sauce.

"Scallops," she ventured. "But square cut and more solid, thicker..."

After prodding one, she'd just pierced it with a fork and held it up for scrutiny, when the other diners began to fade in and out of the candlelit walls. She blinked and blinked again, but to no avail – the room was a blur. And what had previously been a low hum of conversation had now become a loud hypnotic drone. It drowned out all coherent thoughts and her mind numbed. Was she drunk? All of a sudden? She felt herself sway alarmingly. The floor rocked and her fork clattered to the plate.

"I think I need some water."

His voice came from the end of a drainpipe and his face swam before her. "Try it, go on! I can't wait for you to tell me what you think it is."

She took a deep breath, then picked up the fork again. The room was spinning, white-clothed tables whizzing around on a carousel. Trying desperately to focus on the pierced morsel, she angled it towards her mouth. She shouldn't have had that last glass of wine: small it may have been, but it'd been one too many. Best to eat something.

She chewed and swallowed. "I don't know. Unusual. A bit chewy. I really need some water, actually."

"Nice, though?"

She cut another piece. "Quite meaty, almost like rabbit, gamey but–"

"Try a bit more."

She cut another but could not coordinate fork to mouth no matter how hard she tried, and the clash of silver with fine bone china was a cacophony that ricocheted around the room. Nor was it her imagination - everyone had noticed.

"I honestly don't know what it is. The sauce is very unusual, too. Kind of tangy, almost metallic." It had lodged in her throat and she tried to smile. "I've got to be honest, sorry, but I can't say I like it that much. It's too...I don't know, odd. I can't place it."

He shrugged. "What a shame. But the good news is more for me. Pass your plate while no one's looking."

Swapping her plate for his empty one she cast around for the waiter. The room tipped on its axis and she gripped the chair. Why wasn't there any water on the table?

"It was a nice thought, anyway," she said. "So are you going to tell me what it is? Put me out of my misery? I need water, by the way. Seriously."

"Nope. You're going to have to guess, and by the end of the evening I guarantee you'll have it right."

"Emu?"

"Don't be outrageous."

"Parrot."

"Hilarious!"

He laughed, wolfing down the other two chunks and

mopping up the sauce. He ate with total concentration and an almost maniacal fervour. Whatever the delicacy was he certainly couldn't get enough of it, she thought, his attention for the first time that evening not on her, and not on his own performance, but on the morsels in the sauce. Of which there was a tiny globule now stuck to his chin.

"Wow, well whatever it is, you obviously love it."

He dabbed at the corners of his mouth, swallowed a gulp of wine, and nodded. "Delish. And you still don't know what it is, do you?"

His eyes were glinting, and she tried to guess repeatedly but met with no success.

"Wil, I'm sorry but I must have some water. I know I've not had much wine, but I'll never drive down all those hair pin bends in the dark without going over the edge if–"

"Lauren, you cannot even contemplate driving. I told you, we'll get a taxi and another in the morning to collect the cars. Relax. Enjoy. Life is sweet and we're having a wonderful evening."

"I'd still like some water, though. Unless you want me to fall off my perch. Could be embarrassing."

He looked around and where there had been none, a waiter now miraculously appeared. "Water for the lady, please."

"Oh, you said you'd tell me a little more about the castles around here, do you remember? I heard there are more castles along this border than anywhere else in the world."

"Welsh keeping out the English or the English keeping out the Welsh?"

She put it to him that the druids and Celts had been pushed back by the Romans.

"Wherever did you get that notion?"

A bottle of water arrived and gratefully she sank half a glass. He was watching her. Something in his tone had changed. Why? What had she said? Not that she cared hugely. In fact, she really couldn't remember any of the conversation at all, come to think of it. What had they talked about?

Shrugging, she drank the rest of the water, leant forward, and then to her complete surprise an unstoppable torrent of words poured out. Yes, it was her voice ringing out loud and clear, a voice to captivate an audience, to hold court, almost at town crier decibel level. Out came the feeling that the old battles were not as they seemed, and that both sides had been set up - mass sacrifices by old war lords, she felt. She went on to talk about the hangings of old, and the creepy hooded creatures on the hill. Oh, and then there was the ghostly magnetic forest and the black lake, a sort of energy vortex. "It's as if there's a time warp here. I never used to believe in ghosts but if you think about it – how arrogant for us to say that when in truth we don't know what happens to the soul," she said, as coffee was brought and their fellow diners swirled into a kaleidoscope of colours.

There was a slight pause.

"Wow. Gosh. My mother's into that kind of thing, actually."

"Ooh, that coffee's good. Hits the spot. Really?"

"Yes, she's someone who can actually see spirits, though."

He was waiting for her to go on.

But something inside her halted the rolling ball

She took another couple of sips of coffee. "How

interesting."

"Yes, I think you'd get on amazingly well, actually. In fact…" He glanced at his watch. "She might still be up if we scoot off now."

His words were a crossbow shot that caught her off guard, and she struggled to comprehend. "Catch her? Your mother? Sorry, I thought you were staying with your uncle. Didn't you say your uncle was Lord Landgrave?"

He looked bemused. "I think you must have misheard, darling. No, Lord Landgrave's my father."

"Oh." She tried to recall but the conversation in the pub was now vague. There'd been something about his parents leaving him at a boarding school and he was grateful he'd got an uncle. Yes, that was it. She hadn't got it wrong.

"Must be all the cider you had."

"Well–"

He began to stand up. "Extra strong. And then you drove home in the fog. I'm certainly not going to put you at risk like that again. Come on, I'll drive us home. I know the way like the back of my hand."

***

PART THREE

'The devil's agents may be flesh and blood, may they not?'

Arthur Conan Doyle. The Hounds of the Baskervilles.

CHAPTER TWENTY-ONE

The car was powering into thick fog, trees sped past the passenger window, and Lauren was momentarily jolted awake. Citrus and sandalwood scented the hot stuffy air, and trying to keep her head still she swallowed down the taste of wasabi and garlic. Why on earth did she feel so bad? One flute of champagne and two or three tasters of wine was all she'd had, and that was over several courses.

Soon be back at the cottage. Mustn't be sick, mustn't be sick...

Blanking out, a roar of acceleration brought her round again a few minutes later. She stared ahead. A ribbon of eerily lit tarmac was careering towards them. They must be travelling as fast as a jet screaming down a runway for take-off. Her stomach lifted in synchronicity with the car as it shot along the rollercoaster road, and she gripped the edges of the seat, squinting blindly into the wall of fog. He couldn't possibly be able to see - the glare from the headlights was a white haze - yet they were doing at least eighty on the straight.

From under heavy eye lids she looked over. Wil's right hand was on the red leather steering wheel, his left resting on the gear lever as he changed down and touched the brake on the approach to a sharp bend, before accelerating hard again. The road twisted and turned interminably, and all she could do was hold on tightly, making sure to keep her head absolutely level. Eventually the slalom gave way to a steep ascent and the fog thickened further as the car began to climb.

Dizziness kept her from thinking clearly.

They seemed to be sitting very far apart.

What an extraordinarily wide car!

I don't remember getting in it…

And just as it occurred to her how oddly disconnected it felt to be facing imminent death, and that it could happen at any moment, a track from Enigma suddenly blasted out, the base thundering into the car on surround sound. The effect on the heart was the bang of a defibrillator and both of them jumped.

The music evoked the image of a horse-drawn carriage flying at breakneck speed through a fairy tale forest - thousands of acres covered with ancient woodland, mountain streams, remote monasteries and castles. It was hauntingly, pulse-racingly, eerie.

'Je te desire…Prends moi…'

"Did you put that on?" he shouted, immediately reaching for the computer on the dashboard.

She found her mouth didn't work the way it should, the words embarrassingly slurred.

"No, I can't even see it, the um...Bluetooth thing…"

"Someone's been messing with it."

She looked across at him again. In the darkness of the car, lit by neon blue light, the sinews of his face had tightened, eyes granite-hard. With the rare chance to examine his profile, she noticed how deeply etched the mandibular lines actually were – something not noticed head on. His jaw had set to stone.

"Bloody kids. Probably Quinn."

Quinn?

In the far recess of her mind a picture rose unbidden of the dark lake, and the dream she'd had on the first night she'd arrived.

'Kids' he'd said, as had Glynis.

There'd been someone else with the young girl on the path in front of the lake, a figure stepping out moments before the humming started, and she'd tried desperately to wake up.

Prends moi…

Lauren closed her eyes. There'd definitely been someone else there. Another child? Were they real, then? It sounded like it. But…

"I would never have picked this crap. Can you turn it off? That button in front of you."

The sound was amplifying by the second, the base beat reverberating through every cell of the body. He had both hands on the wheel as he manoeuvred a hair pin bend before flying down the middle of the road at electrifying speed. How much had he had to drink? She thought back. Certainly he'd drunk most of the champagne, but also each glass of wine that arrived - she'd only sampled them but he'd knocked the whole lot straight down. And didn't he say they'd get a taxi?

What had happened?

Not only could she not recall getting into the car, but there was no memory of even crossing the car park, of the sweet fresh breath of night air on her face as they left the restaurant. Nothing!

The instrumental track now broke into a series of breathy gasps, a female panting, and then it stopped and a man's deadpan voice delivered each word precisely: '*The sky turned dark…the sun went black…*'

Staring straight ahead, she frowned at the computer board.

"There," he said. "The one you're looking at."

She hit the power button and the music died. Back to the throbbing roar of the engine.

So how come he isn't drunk?

The digital display showed eighty-seven, eighty-eight, over ninety…

They were going to die. And her entire body was rigid with that expectation, when at long last the sign with the jaunty, foot-tapping fiddler floated through the fog. Fiddlers Elbow. Her hopes leapt at the sight of it. Five more minutes and this would be over. She would rush through the front door, lock it, down a pint of water and then fall straight into bed. In many ways, she thought, it had been a truly wonderful evening, but now it felt as if she'd just come round from an anaesthetic. The nausea was hot and came in waves. She began to fantasise about the sleeping bag and the cold cocoon that was Clingbine Cottage, and with her foot she nudged the patent clutch bag on the floor, itching to pick it up, to get the key in her hand ready. She'd have to bolt from the car and shoot inside as fast as possible.

"Hangman's noose," said Wil as they hared towards the junction.

"What?"

Tapping the brake he changed down and swung the wheel hard right.

For a fragment of a second as the car turned, she was convinced her head had separated from the rest of her body.

"It's what they used to call that place, 'Hangman's Noose.'"

"Fiddlers Elbow?"

"Watch!"

The face of the same swinging corpse she'd seen two days before, lurched at the passenger window, and this time she got a much closer and clearer look. The eyes were wide open, partly pecked out and rotting, the mouth a howling cavern; and lower down, where the body should be, his guts were spilling out like a dead black mamba.

She leapt back as the car swung round. "Fuck!"

Wil laughed. "Not everyone can see them. Whole place is riddled with ghosts. They used to hang horse thieves and traitors at the crossroads. Served them right."

She tried to recover enough to answer. The entire evening meal - trout, spring onions, pak choi, truffles – was swilling up into her throat, and she swallowed repeatedly, forcing down what was determined to be ejected. To hit the wall.

"As a warning?"

"Always."

She tried to breathe through her nose only. "I've seen that one before actually, a couple of days ago, although I didn't get erm, such a close a look as just now."

"The lower astral is a fascinating topic, isn't it? All those trapped in eternal ignorance and torture. You were most informative tonight, by the way."

Was I?

"I can hardly remember what I said. To be honest, I'll be glad to get back. I must have had more to drink than I thought."

The car now shot up the track towards Groom Lake.

Nearly there…two minutes…less…

"You really do know your way blindfolded. How can you possibly see the road?"

"My family home."

The information took a moment to permeate, a blunt knife, delayed impact. He had definitely said D'Avranches Grange was his uncle's. So why had that story changed to Lord Landgrave being his father? And why had he made out she'd originally misheard, when he'd gone to some length to tell the story about not being collected from boarding school? The story had actually caused her to recall it.

Or had she misheard? It was impossible to be sure now. And perhaps the cider she'd ordered at the pub wasn't the low alcohol one she'd asked for, but a high strength one and the barman had made a mistake? Wil could be right. To be fair she'd been extremely stressed recently and possibly wasn't remembering things correctly.

They passed under the point where the arch of trees closed overhead, and began to race downhill. Her eyes flitted from him to the ford just as water sprayed the windows. The view then cleared and at long last the gates to the estate emerged from the fog.

Lauren began reaching for the seat belt clip as they levelled with the posts. "Brilliant. Thank you ever so much. I'll sort a taxi tomor–"

He accelerated straight past with his foot flat to the board, and sped up the drive to the house as if she hadn't spoken.

"Erm…?"

"Come in for a few minutes. They're dying to meet

you."

It happened so fast - from the long tree-lined driveway to the gravelled courtyard – that he'd parked before she even had chance to respond.

Stunned, she unclipped her seatbelt in silence. Wil switched off the engine. The interior of the car was dark, the night squally with foggy rain. He turned in his seat.

"What's the matter? Don't tell me you're shy? Not you! Not after tonight."

Her eyes were gritty beneath leaden lids and the words came out in a jumble. "No, it's just I don't feel a hundred percent. A bit sick. It's okay, I'll walk back."

She glanced at the archway, and the long black snake of the drive behind. A flurry of leaves blew against the side of the car.

Why were they dying to meet her? This dazzling, wealthy man must have taken out hundreds of women in his time, and as he'd said himself they'd been some of the most beautiful in the world – many of them titled and famous. So why on earth would his family be dying to meet someone like her – an ordinary ex-nurse of no fixed abode?

Their eyes locked.

"Come and have a coffee. I honestly don't want the evening to end, that's all." He leaned forward and gently kissed her cheek.

And then to her utter amazement a voice she barely recognised said, "All right, thank you. A coffee would be lovely."

***

Chapter Twenty-Two

All the bedrooms overlooked the courtyard, behind each window a palatial suite with a double aspect and a balcony. It was far more imposing than imagined, Lauren thought, as they walked towards a stone porch. Wood smoke laced the foggy night air, and as they neared Wil gave her hand a squeeze before stepping inside. About to follow, however, she glanced up at the darkened windows. Although the upper floors were unlit, she could have sworn there'd been someone watching their arrival - a small pale face not dissimilar to the ones seen at the mill. But on second glance there was no one there.

The little fish hook snagged inside again, as she looked over her shoulder at the archway and the vast expanse of night behind it, before turning to face the studded oak door to the house. Smoothly and soundlessly it opened from within.

The hallway resembled that of a castle, with walls several feet thick and a large inglenook fireplace. The flames threw an amber glow across polished floorboards, and feeling watched, Lauren started slightly at the sight of several suits of armour on the staircase. Family ancestors peered out of life-size oil cavasses, and animal heads adorned almost every available space. There were a lot of embalmed creatures, she noticed: in display cabinets, over the fireplace, and skins lying across the floor.

So, she'd been right – it was a hunting lodge?

No one spoke, and the house echoed with the sound of their footsteps as the woman who'd mutely answered the door - so inconspicuous in her uniform of black blouse and skirt as to be rendered invisible - now led them deeper inside.

Wil immediately set off at a pace and Lauren's heart picked up a beat. She needed the bathroom pretty urgently, but the other two were already quite far ahead. And all sets of feet, including her own, were chopping into the floorboards in a rapid march through hollow rooms filled with dead animals. It looked like a museum, she was thinking, with its deathly almost reverential hush, and only the occasional lamp to light the way. How much further was it? She really did need the bathroom, but yet another set of doors had been opened and she was struggling to keep up. Why the bloody rush? And where on earth were they going? It wasn't until they'd reached the far end of the house, however, the room furthest from the entrance, that she found out.

Muffled voices sounded from beyond the final set of double doors, and she tried to make her brain function better. What a massive disadvantage to be introduced to people for the first time when her mind was as thick as a custard tart. And Wil was completely silent, hadn't once checked to see if she was even still here. Was he the same man who, less than an hour ago, had been regaling her with anecdotes, and not to put too fine a point on it, compliments? The same one who'd just told her he didn't want the evening to end?

Anyway, it was no use because she absolutely had to go to the bathroom.

"Excuse me, Wil..." Her voice ricocheted around the

cavernous hall and she faltered. "I'm sorry, but I really need to–"

Unexpectedly, he grabbed her hand as the doors were pushed open. And completely unprepared she found herself thrust straight in. The leading role without a script!

There was a draught from the doors as they were swiftly closed behind, the only sound that of a fire crackling in the grate. She blinked. The family appeared to be in semi-darkness, the scene a blur of flickering, shadowy walls and blank staring faces.

'Lamps,' Lauren thought. 'Lamps with red shades. People not together…dotted around…positioned so I can't see them all at once.'

"Here we are," said Wil. "Dolly, Todd – this is the lovely lady staying in our cottage, Lauren Stafford." He had a hand on the small of her back, pushing her firmly into the room.

She had absolutely no idea what to say. Was the one he called 'Dolly' his mother? Why would he call his parents by their first names?

Confused, she smiled. "Hello!"

Without replying, Dolly Landgrave eyed her from where she sat by the fire nursing a glass of sherry. With steel grey hair coiffed into something Princess Anne would sport, she wore a long, red tartan skirt and a camel polo neck sweater. Absolutely no question, Lauren decided - Dolly was the one holding court.

The others in the room, appraising her from a variety of different angles, included an older man in a white suit hovering on the periphery, and a bald man playing chess with a flaxen haired boy of about twelve. Red shoes again, she noted. How odd. Why red shoes? She could not recall ever seeing men in red shoes before tonight.

"We've had a fab evening up at Folly Point," said Wil. "So I thought we'd pop back and have a nightcap with you. That all right, Dolly?"

Dolly hadn't taken her eyes off Lauren. A slight smile twitched one side of a somewhat horsey looking mouth. "What fun! So tell me, my dear, how did you enjoy the evening?"

The heat inside the room was insufferable, and annoyingly a deep flush was beginning to suffuse her face. Someone smelled as if their skin was saturated in port, and had steeped in it for days.

Nodding, she tried to form the words, to say, "It was lovely, thank you." But what actually came out she couldn't be sure.

The boy who'd been concentrating on the game of chess now raised his head and steadily regarded her, his eyes cool blue, features pointed and narrow.

Something was off. There was a stilted unnatural atmosphere, as if she'd interrupted something and they were deciding what to do about that.

"And what about the surprise dish?" Dolly was saying. "Did you manage to guess what it was, dear?"

She'd almost forgotten about it, but the re-conjured memory of glue-like morsels floating in grey garlicky sauce, almost made her stomach eject it there and then. It was stifling in here, the heat at near furnace temperature. Were all the radiators on? There was a huge fire at the opposite end of the room, too. Determined to ask if she might use the bathroom before she spontaneously combusted, Lauren attempted to answer.

"No, I'm afraid not. Look, I'm really sorry but would it

be–?"

Wil put a hand on the small of her back, this time shoving her pretty forcefully. It was such a surprise she stopped speaking altogether. He was manoeuvring her towards a chair opposite his mother, and stunned, she found herself being seated by the fire.

The two women faced each other.

Dolly observed her without expression and Lauren steeled herself. What the hell was coming? Why did she feel so incredibly uneasy? And would no one offer her a drink? A glass of cold water would really help. She was beginning to feel ill, as if coming down with something. Where was the woman in the black uniform? She scanned the room. Maybe none of these people ever poured anyone else a drink? They were all so statue still, fading in and out, the man in the white suit by the window mutely observing, the others non-descript and silent. The boy at the chessboard was now focusing on the game again, but just as she was about to turn back to Dolly, his opponent, the bald man, glanced up sharply.

Nothing could have prepared her.

His photograph had been a weak copy.

The shape of Lord Landgrave's eyes - upside down half-moons - was distinguishable enough, but in reality they were as tar black as Groom Lake. There came from within not one glimmer of light. And as she unwillingly stared back, it was as if something inside of him stepped aside, and an inquisitive alter intelligence appeared, shifting and stirring within the fixed, leaden eyes.

Like the shapes on the bottom of the lake.

Abruptly, Lauren turned to face Dolly.

Close up, she was much older than the initial

impression, the illusion of youth largely due to stretched skin and flashing button eyes.

"Are we going to put her out of her misery?" she asked, staring straight at Lauren but speaking to the room at large.

"Go easy on her," said Wil. "It's always a shock and she might never forgive me."

Dolly's mouth crinkled at the corners.

"Do forgive Wil's incorrigible teasing. So how are you finding Groom Lake? We simply had no idea anyone was staying in the old cottage."

"It's not what I hoped for," Lauren blurted out. "The cottage, I mean."

"Would you like a drink? A sherry, perhaps?"

Lauren smiled with relief. They were human, after all! "Oh, yes please. Thank you. Tonic water with ice would be wonderful, thank you."

It arrived in an instant, wordlessly handed to her in a crystal glass.

"And in what way does our ghastly little cottage fall short?"

Lauren downed half the glass, then oddly found herself continuing to shoot from the hip. "To be honest it's pretty dismal. Damp and cold as a crypt." She drained the rest. "I actually asked Glynis for my money back."

Did I just say that?

"Oh, poor you. Then you must stay with us, mustn't she, Wil? Arrange a room for her, Davis."

The order was given without looking at the faceless, voiceless woman in the black uniform. And as Lauren cast around for the woman called, 'Davis,' the boy at the chessboard glanced over his shoulder again. This time their gaze met, in the shaded rosy light of the lamp. Both of his eye sockets were badly bruised.

"Erm, oh no, it's quite all right. I didn't mean…I mean I really couldn't. I'd rather not, but thank you anyway."

"We wouldn't hear of you being uncomfortable here, especially when we enjoy such…" Dolly waved a red-jewelled hand around. "…luxury."

"You're very kind but no, honestly. I'd prefer to stay in the cottage."

"Lauren darling, we won't hear of it." Wil's voice floated around like a stray balloon as the walls began to fold inwards. "We had absolutely no idea it was so dire for you."

She clutched the chair to stop herself from falling. This was what had happened at the restaurant only far, far worse. Without warning the glass fell from a hand that no longer had any kind of grip, hitting the rug with a dull thud.

"You look slightly ill, dear," said Dolly, holding her gaze. "You know, you really shouldn't have meddled."

"Maybe it's something she ate?"

Laughter bounced off the panelling and swirled around inside her head. The tonic…aniseed…

"Davis, take her to the Tudor room."

"No, really–"

But her feet no longer touched the ground and the bed was spinning.

Bed?

"Did anyone tell her it was human flesh?"

"Do you think she's acquired the taste?"

Bed? What bed?

***

Chapter Twenty-Three

From under heavy eyelids Lauren tried to make sense of her surroundings. The room was gloomy, lit only by a lamp on the dresser opposite. She forced herself awake. The embossed wallpaper was the colour of dried blood, and over the fireplace another bulbous-eyed ancestor, this one with an elongated skull, stared blankly out of an oil painting. She was lying in a king size four poster, and long velvet curtains had been left undrawn either side of French windows. But it was what adorned both the ebony dresser and a chest of drawers that captured her attention. They wavered and shimmied in and out of focus, but there was no mistake. They were snakes!

She leapt up. But her body did not. And the panic was a horse kick.

What the fuck?

What was this? She was totally paralysed. Was this a waking nightmare again? Like in the cottage? She could wake up at any moment, right? However, there was no sense of dreaming. Wide eyed she checked every detail of the room.

No, it's fucking real!

And none of her limbs would move.

Adrenalin squeezed her heart and a cold sweat broke out, even as her eyelids began to drop - such was the lead weight. Her tongue was stuck too, wedged at the back of her throat, caked in concrete. The only part of her that seemed to work was her eyesight. Beyond the lamp on the dresser, at the far end of the bedroom, was a smaller room surrounded by full length mirrors. The mirrors glinted slightly from moonlight through the windows - lead windows. And now that she noticed them she realised mirrors were everywhere, all around the room, including one overhead, facing down from the canopy of the four poster.

Falling into something soft and downy…dreamy…smiling…a mirror dancing high above…

Sleep was dragging her down and she began to drift away. Just as something moved in the umbra of the shadows and she forced her eyes open again. But she could not sustain concentration a second longer, or move if indeed she was awake. Instead, the deep coma of the drugged pulled her back into its depths. And what unfolded next defied all belief.

At first it was a vague awareness.

There were murmurs of what sounded like encouragement, "Oh yes, yes definitely… come *on*!"

The scent of a heady fragrance hung in the air – musky, tangy, sweet – and tongues of candlelight flickered in the mirrors.

Mirrors!

Her eyes snapped open to see her naked body reflected in the mirror above - splayed out, ankles and wrists tied at four points. How long had this been going on? Many hands were on her, touching, pushing and caressing, voices hissing and murmuring. She shut her eyes in an attempt to block out the scene. This wasn't real. Soon she would wake. But a man was stroking her hair, breathing heavily into her neck, and with shame she felt her body arch, rising to meet his.

Was it Wil Landgrave? Was she drunk? Had he come to her room? She lay motionless, staring up into the glass mirror, unable to prevent what was happening or utter a single sound, as full comprehension dawned. The man who'd undressed her and who'd been caressing her for possibly hours was not Wil Landgrave, but an elderly man with a spiny, hairy back and an unnaturally elongated head covered with liver spots.

The one over the fireplace in the oil painting!

She opened her mouth to scream, a silent scream, as blood then spurted from her lip, the membrane punctured as if by the fang of a snake. The piercing pop released a warm spout of her life force and suddenly everywhere there were snakes - coiling up the bedstead, writhing out of the wallpaper, slithering over the floor and pulsating across the sheets. The hiss of cobras filled the air, vipers flicked tongues at her face, and the muscular weight of a python oozed across her chest.

Get out of my head!

Stop!

Instinctively she prayed, calling on God and all His angels, on Jesus Christ, on Archangel Michael, and all that was divine and benevolent. If there was evil then there was good. Squeezing her eyes tightly shut, she remembered with blinding clarity a day at the beach, a blue sky day when as a child she'd run delightedly into the sparkling ocean, the only holiday Auntie Claire had ever taken her on. She was transported in an instant, could see and feel it so clearly – the rhythmic ebb and flow of the waves, the shock of the cold sea around her waist and the grains of sand swirling beneath. Time stood still for her then, the summer breeze dancing with flecks of gold. If she was to die here, if that's what this was, then let it be with this memory and not in terror.

"Lauren, go back!"

The white glare of the day was dazzling. She brought her hands up to her eyes to shield them. But just at the moment she moved them away, to turn and see who'd called her name, she woke with a bang in the chest. And the woman's voice faded.

They'd been speaking at length, had a conversation she felt sure, but the memory had already gone. Except for one phrase. And that had been, 'Pay attention!'

She dipped in and out of consciousness, floating into repeated scenes, the bedroom full of whispers, hisses, and distant chanting.

"She's awake."

"She doesn't remember."

"Give her some more."

"We don't want her dead."

Eventually the voices faded and when she next came round there was a definite feeling it was morning. The night was over.

Could she move?

Her tongue, previously wedged fast, now came unstuck and she swallowed what felt like a ball of glue, eyes straining into the grey dawn. But she could move her fingers! She flexed each one. Then tried her toes, legs and arms. So was that a drug induced nightmare? Or had it actually happened?

Hardly daring to find out she worked through the details of her surroundings. There, in front, was indeed an ebony dressing table, although there weren't any snakes slithering over it. A violent recollection of the room being full of serpents caused her to grab at the sheets and scan every square inch. No snakes. Thank God. But there were mirrors lining the walls, and her reflection was looking down at her.

What about the man? The one who'd been…? She made herself look at the portrait over the fireplace. And quieted her heart.

So when did he spike my drink? Oh my God, I've messed up. Terribly. Horribly. I knew it was all wrong and yet I still did it. Why, though? To be fucking polite? Because I thought someone wealthy and good looking would take care of me? What a fool! What a massive, massive fool!

Closing her eyes, she silently pleaded with God, acutely aware the whole place, and the house itself, was one of abject darkness. You could almost hear the hum of low discordant frequency.

Pay attention!

What could she do? Was it remotely possible to get out?

With a jolt she suddenly remembered the sight of her spread-eagled body tied with restraints, and her hands shot under the covers. Naked. She was absolutely naked. In panic she examined her wrists. No marks, though. Then felt the rest of her body, down to the ankles. No damage. No pain.

So what had happened, then? Drugs? An opiate-fuelled bad trip?

The confusion was terrible, the not knowing, the messing with her mind, her sanity. Like someone shipwrecked, finding themselves cast onto the high seas, she calmed her nerves, adjusting to the enormity of the situation. There would be a solution, a way out, had to be.

So where were her clothes? And who had undressed her? Perhaps she and Wil really had…?

Shame flushed her neck and cheeks right up to the ear lobes as a memory of the mirror scene resurfaced. Surely not? Besides there was no pain, no damage. It was hard to think, to make her brain work through the fog, and she blanked out. Momentarily? A few minutes? Or hours?

Because when she woke up again the lamp had been lit. Was it evening already?

And a young girl was sitting on the side of the bed.

***

CHAPTER TWENTY-FOUR

They stared at each other.

I've seen you before.

Lauren blinked and blinked again. Was she a ghost or real? The girl was so ethereally pale, the skin almost translucent, with a map of indigo veins at the temples and beneath her eyes.

A vague memory surfaced of the child in the mac and wellingtons on the path leading to the lake. Was this the same one who'd appeared in her dream? Were she and the boy, Quinn, the ones the Moodys had referred to as difficult kids? Had they smashed her windows? Was Quinn the boy playing chess last night?

She thought fast. If this was the same girl, and she had a feeling it was, then all the child could have seen on that lake path, was an empty space. Yet she'd stared at her as if they'd met in person, strangers in the middle of the woods in the dark and rain.

"Hello!"

Lauren tried to respond to the image that swam before her. But her lips were caked dry, the words sticking to the roof of her mouth. She swallowed a couple of times and had another go. "Hello!"

"You're Lauren."

"Yes. Who are you?"

"Hermia."

Lauren nodded. Was she talking to a ghost or was the girl alive?

"Do you live here?"

Hermia's wraith like face bobbed before her, fading in and out, as she continued to stare down at Lauren. It was almost as if she was attempting to communicate telepathically, her round blue eyes willing information into Lauren. Stone still and without speaking, she shimmered in a bluish haze. She must be so cold in the chilly night air, Lauren thought. And far too young to be out of bed, let alone wandering in the woods on her own at night.

"Are you all right?"

Hermia wasn't moving, had frozen.

"Hermia?"

The trance broke at the sound of her name and Hermia's expression cleared. Jolted into life she checked over her shoulder at the closed door, then leaned forwards and whispered conspiratorially, "Do you want to see your dress?"

"What?"

"For tomorrow night. You're going to be the guest of honour."

"What do you mean?"

"In the supreme temple."

"What supreme temple?"

"It's the mother supreme council of the whole world, and it's full of ancient things from Egypt. There's a huge pointed pillar inside, an open stone casket, and painted mummies like you'd see in a museum; and a massive statue like a man but with a goat's head. I've only been in once so I don't remember anymore. It was too dark."

"Hang on, where is this temple?"

Hermia's eyes flicked to the door behind again. "Shhh! It's in the woods."

Lauren's heart missed a beat as full comprehension sank in. Nothing about this conversation was in any way normal. She was effectively homeless and had no living relatives. Homeless people went missing. Children without parents went missing... She tried to lever herself up on one elbow, but found her limbs were too heavy, her head lolled backwards and she almost blacked out.

Hermia, however, seemed almost feverishly excited.

"There's a special play being performed. It's on the Autumn Equinox to celebrate the harvest. And afterwards we all go up to the top of the hill, to the cave."

She thought fast. If she feigned ignorance maybe Hermia would say more? God, her mouth and throat were desperately dry, her head thudding dully on the crown.

"What does being a guest of honour entail exactly? What do I have to do?"

"Nothing really. You don't have to do anything. It's just tradition to give a sacrifice to the goat god so the rest of the people can live, and then there'll be a good harvest and great wealth. It's for the kingdom. It's just a play, not real. I'm going to be a human altar."

She badly wanted to be sick. Waves of horror rose in one tidal surge.

Hermia seemed to predict the need, her glance flicking to a bowl on the bedside table.

Lauren grabbed it.

"It'll be the medicine. Have some water."

It was an acidic retch that burned the throat, and after a minute she put the bowl down and picked up the glass of water.

"It's okay. Drink it."

"I have to get out of here."

Again, Hermia checked the door was shut, then shook her head. "Why?"

"Look, who are you? Are you living here? Where did you come from?"

"Me and Quinn were fostered. My mum died and my dad didn't want me because I was trouble. So they put me in Robin's Nest, a children's home. No one knows where Quinn came from though, including him. There are others but they're mostly up at the mill."

Robin's Nest? The name seemed oddly familiar.

She shook her head. "Others at the mill?"

Hermia raised her eyes to the ceiling, doing an imaginary inventory. "Umm… Spike, Badger….no, he's gone now… um, Snout, Puck and I think, Keeper and Watch are still there."

"Still there? Gone? What do you mean?"

Hermia shrugged. "I don't know. Sometimes people are rewarded, and other times they get punishments if they're trouble. Bad trouble. No one wants that."

"Who else knows you're here?"

"Who else? What do you mean?"

"I mean, no one else knows you're here, then? No family–"

"Just like you," said Hermia.

Lauren's heart did a little flip. "Actually they do." She grasped at the only straw there was. "I have a friend nearby. I'm only staying overnight here because I had a tad too much to drink. So do you know where my clothes are, Hermia? I'd really like to get up and dressed."

Hermia gestured towards a row of glossy, ebony closets with gold catches. "I think Davis put your dress in there. You can see it if you like? It's very pretty–"

"Thank you."

As Hermia walked over to the wardrobe, she pictured herself running flat out down the long tree-lined drive. This could not be real. My God, why hadn't she thought to tell Wil that Hannah planned to call in next day? Actually, come to think of it, how long had she been here? What was it now - the twenty-fourth or twenty-fifth of October? How many days was it before the Halloween party she now realised was a sacrificial ceremony?

Suppressing a rise of panic, Lauren again struggled to sit up, her head like a goldfish bowl full of swilling water, as Hermia pulled a hanger off the rail. Were the outside doors locked, she wondered? What about the one to the courtyard? How about the French doors opening onto the balcony? Was there a way down from here?

"You can only look at it," said Hermia, holding up the dress. "Don't touch because it needs to be perfect. You have to bathe in rosewater first before you put it on. But not until tomorrow."

It was long, plain, and white. Virginal white linen.

"You said Halloween. So by my calculations I have five or six days yet? Thing is, I want to go back to the cottage and get some clean clothes before then. I also want to see the friend I told you about. I can come back for the play."

Hermia's face and voice softened, her demeanour dreamy. "No, it's Halloween tomorrow. And don't worry because we've been washing you, me and Davis. And giving you the medicine on a spoon." She screwed up her face. "It's called the Brompton Mixture. It's to just make you like things more, to not feel any pain. It's nice and you swallowed it down so you seemed to like it and–"

They both froze at the sudden sound of voices in the corridor outside, and the soft pad of footsteps on thick pile rugs.

Fixated on the door, Lauren hissed, "Start brushing my hair or something." She met Hermia's gaze and trying to calm her thumping heart, used what was possibly the one chance she had to make Hermia do what she said. "We don't want you to get into trouble."

Trouble...

My God, Lauren thought, what terrors did that word conjure for this poor kid?

A dark cloud shifted behind Hermia's eyes, but it had done the trick. Without hesitation she sped over to the wardrobe, replaced the dress, and closed the doors so gently there was barely a sigh of air. Light and quick of foot she flew back to the dresser for the hairbrush, and no sooner had her hand clasped around the pearl handle when the footsteps paused directly by the bedroom door.

Neither of them drew breath

From somewhere deep within the cavern of the house a clock chimed, the moment lasting for what seemed like all eternity.

And then whoever it was continued on their way.

Hermia was holding the brush mid-air. "They're going to the chamber," she whispered.

"What chamber?"

She did not reply, still holding the brush - on freeze-frame.

"Hermia? What chamber?"

No response.

Lauren frowned. "Hermia!"

The girl jumped and swung to face her. "What? No, shush! Be quiet. I have to go."

"What chamber, Hermia?"

She had, Lauren thought, observing the deathly pallor of her skin, the fragility of a captured songbird.

"It's a secret. I'm not supposed to know. Don't say anything."

"It's okay. I promise I won't tell anyone."

After a moment's indecision, Hermia then lunged towards her unexpectedly, and levelling with Lauren's ear, whispered so quietly her words were almost inaudible.

"I listen in a lot. I can do this thing sometimes, not always, but sometimes I leave my body and float around. I can hear and see things in other rooms or outside. Not clearly. But when I wake up I remember. So I remembered..."

The child pulled back and looked deeply into her eyes, searching her face.

"Ah! Oh, I see."

"You understand?"

Lauren nodded. "What did you remember?"

Hermia leaned close again. "That they said no one could remote view in there. That's what they said – remote view. It's below ground, under the lodge in the woods. They get to it through a tunnel. I think it's where they take the men to do their special vows. That's later today."

"Have you ever told them you can do that?" Lauren whispered back. "That your mind can float around outside the body?"

She shook her head.

"Don't! I'm deadly serious. If they know you can do

that, and that you have the sight I have a feeling you'll be in mortal danger."

She frowned. "Like you?"

"Sorry?"

"Well, you have the sight. I heard them saying."

"What do you–?"

"Shush! He's come back."

"Who–?"

Hermia put her fingers to her lips. "Shh!"

***

Chapter Twenty-Five

There'd been no sound or shadow under the door to warn them. Yet Wil Landgrave now stood framed against the lamp lit corridor. And in that instant, with hair-crawling recoil, Lauren's perception of reality shifted.

His entire demeanour had changed as completely as an actor taking off a costume at the end of a play. There wasn't a trace left of the personality that had so artfully mesmerised her over dinner. But more disturbing than that, far more, was the towering hooded figure in a soot black robe standing behind him. And there were more lining the corridor, a row of them.

"How are you feeling, Lauren?"

Every nerve was firing. She'd never been a good liar, but it felt like a good idea to convince him she was thoroughly stupid. "Exhausted. Every limb's a dead weight. I don't know what's wrong with me, it could be flu, but I can't keep awake. I'm so sorry."

His eyes pierced the gloom like lasers. "Go back to sleep, then. No rush. Take all the time you need."

She yawned as Hermia began to brush her hair again, the strokes gentle, rhythmic, soothing.

"Thank you. You've all been so kind. It's just I can't keep my eyes open."

He did not reply. The towering shape seemed to be

descending on him, casting his face into darkness.

"Wake me if you come back and I'm still asleep. It must be flu. I'm so embarrassed, this is awful."

He continued to observe for an uncomfortably long time. Had she overdone it? Did he suspect she'd twigged?

"Not a problem," he said, eventually. "I'll pop back and check on you later."

After the door had closed behind him, she realised both of them were holding their breaths, Hermia with the brush suspended mid-air. Out in the corridor there came no sound of retreating footfalls. No indication of where he now was or which direction he'd taken.

An age passed before Lauren whispered, "Are my clothes and bag in the wardrobe too, Hermia? Were they with the dress?"

"Yes, why? You can't go. You're not allowed to."

"Of course not," Lauren said quickly. "I was just asking."

Someone with a heavy tread was walking past the door.

"Where's the entrance to the tunnel you mentioned? The one that goes to the chamber?"

"I can't go down to the chamber, I told you."

A memory surfaced of the strange ritual she'd dreamed of, and the man who'd taken a solemn, deathly service. Was that the chamber Hermia spoke of? How come she'd seen it? How could that possibly be?

"None of us know what happens inside there," Hermia was saying. "Maybe I'm not allowed to know."

"But the entrance? Do they access it from the house or from outside?"

"Oh, it's at the end of the corridor here. You come to a turret and go down the iron steps to the tunnel."

She could almost hear the clang of their feet on the rungs. "Thank you. So you mean at the end of this corridor past my room"

"Yes."

"And what time does the meeting start? I just, you know, wouldn't want to miss Wil coming back to check on me...Wouldn't want to...you know, fall asleep."

The words sounded loaded and false to her own ears. She'd never been a good liar.

But Hermia answered with all the innocence of an honest child. "Eight. And there's a supper afterwards. Davis told me. She has to go down there. You mustn't ask me anymore."

"But–"

Hermia had begun to brush Lauren's hair again, humming gently to herself.

"Hermia, just one more question. I don't suppose you know how long they'll be in the chamber? How long does the meeting go on for?"

The humming grew louder, a tuneless blocking-out of everything external.

Through the haze of a drugged stupor, Lauren began to plan her escape. The only method of gauging the time was by the chime of the clock in the hall below. If the meeting started at eight there would likely be no further footsteps outside in the corridor for what - an hour afterwards? Or two?

She flicked a sidelong glance at Hermia as she brushed her hair, humming softly, her fingers deft and light. The effect was hypnotic, and a flash of white as her head lolled, roused her from passing out again.

"Actually, I think I'd better get some rest now," she

said. "What are you doing later this evening while the adults are all in the chamber? Do you watch TV?"

Hermia looked surprised, as though she'd been snapped out of a sleepwalk too quickly. "Um, well, my job is to keep an eye on you when Davis is busy. I have to look after you."

"And is Davis busy?"

"Yes, she's got to greet all the guests and take the supper down. I told you, she's the only one who goes down to the chamber."

Lauren slumped back onto the pillows and yawned again. "I desperately need to sleep, Hermia. So if you want you could take a bit of time off? Aren't you tired, too? Why don't you go and watch a film or get something nice to eat? You know, while the family are all occupied?"

"Um–"

She closed her eyes. "I'll be fast asleep. You don't need to do anything for me at the moment – I've had more than enough of that mixture. I could sleep for a week."

"Yes, all right. It might be good to get some food while they're in there. But I don't want to watch the television, I want to see the guests arriving. My bedroom's over the top of this one so I've got a good view of the courtyard. They're important people, famous people…" Immediately she put a hand to her mouth. "Oh no, I'm not supposed to say who they are."

"No, of course not. Don't worry, I won't tell anyone."

After Hermia had gone, Lauren darted over to the wardrobe and noted with huge relief that all of her belongings were inside.

Pay attention!

Her fuzzy mind was busy. What a strange mixture of knowing and innocence, Hermia had. She must see and hear far more than her young mind could comprehend, yet somehow she'd normalised what was far, far from normal.

You don't have to do anything. It's just tradition to give a sacrifice!

Her clutch bag was exactly as she'd left it, or more precisely dropped it on the floor. And her black dress and coat had been put on hangers. Snatching them, constantly vigilant and half expecting Wil to silently materialise at any moment, she hastily dressed. Then slipped the coat, shoes and bag underneath the bed. It was going to be a case of perfect timing.

Walking over to the window, Lauren stood behind the heavy curtains and peered down at the courtyard below. Who were these illustrious guests and just what did such a secretive meeting entail? So secretive it had to be conducted in a dungeon room sealed from remote viewing. Why would they be concerned about such a rare and controversial possibility as that? It was akin to war cabinet secrecy and the generals being worried about ghostly intrusions...

Again her scalp prickled.

Face it! Face what?

But she knew. This was Satanism. And the important people coming here also knew that. She thought again about the man who'd taken the ceremony she'd dreamed about, the one who'd denied Christ, who'd thought that up to that point it was just a play, an all-boys club. Until it wasn't. Until it was real.

***

CHAPTER TWENTY-SIX

A black Bentley crunched across the gravel, parking close to the same dimly lit porch Lauren had entered several nights ago. She squinted into the darkness. Another slick car using the back entrance to the house! Why did no one use the grand driveway at the front – the one flanked by open fields and majestic oaks? Why did they all come this way?

The second it stopped, a uniformed chauffeur jumped out and held open a rear door. He stood rigidly to attention as a man subsequently alighted, looking straight ahead without speaking. No word or gesture of acknowledgement passed between them.

It was difficult to see the man in the long overcoat walking smartly inside, especially in such a fleeting moment, but the copious mop of swept-back white hair made him immediately identifiable as a well-known politician. Lauren's eyes widened, as stony faced he hurried into the porch. She wasn't certain what position he held, but he featured regularly in the media. 'Tipped to be the next prime minister', was a phrase often touted, a man renowned for his personal charm and friendly banter: 'One of the people.' 'The people's choice!'

The sky had briefly cleared to reveal a speckled canvas of stars brushed with sweeping clouds, and the wind was whipping up again. The moon was almost full, and the silvery canopy of trees on the lower reaches of the forest bounced and swayed in periodic gusts. After the Bentley had retreated down the drive, Lauren's gaze drifted over to the woods. You couldn't see the lake from here, but there was a clear path trailing into the woods from the house - a moonlit thread that faded in and out of focus depending on the whim of the clouds.

At first she didn't trust the evidence of her own eyes. Perhaps it had been a trick of the light? But the next time the clouds cleared, the silvery haze of the path was once more revealed and she gasped. One brief glimpse was all there was, but a line of ghostly children was running along it. One and then another...alive or not... bluish tinges in rapid motion...

She had no time to make sense of it, however, because the headlights from a second car now swept over the stone walls of the courtyard, and she stepped back, keeping well out of sight. But at that exact moment, out of the corner of her eye, a figure darted between the trees and her attention flicked back to the path.

Her mouth dropped open.

It was just a flash of an image, a captured echo of the past. But a ghostly figure she recognised was leading a horse into the undergrowth - a woman in a long riding habit pulling at the animal's bridle, her voice a sing-song taunt, "Where are you? Ready or not, I'm coming to get you!"

Lauren's heart did a little skip, remembering the woman seen in the black lake, and the face that was contorted with malice as she lifted up a riding crop to thrash her with. The mocking words were spiked with icy glee, and instinctively Lauren cowered further into the shadow of the room. The ghostly woman's presence had instilled a cold terror she could not explain, and in the tender place where there'd been a snag of fish hook, there was a now a grab. The effect was as if some invisible force had reached inside and tried to pull out her soul. She put both hands over the spot and told herself it was her own fear, that was all. Not real. A ghost couldn't hurt anyone. And when she next looked up the path was shrouded once again in darkness.

The second car had now rolled to a stop in front of the porch and Lauren, with some relief, switched focus as another uniformed chauffeur alighted and a rear door opened.

This man was older than the first, much older, his frame tall and gangly as he walked with the aid of a cane towards the porch. There emanated from him an air of absolute authority, his skeletal appearance that of a man from a bygone age, dressed in a funereal frock coat and a black trilby. As he passed directly underneath the window, she leaned forwards very slightly to see if he was someone she might recognise. At which point he stopped. Abruptly. About to tap the cane to the ground he stood stock still with the stick mid-air. Almost indiscernibly his back had stiffened and his head was cocked to one side. A blackbird listening for a worm.

Don't look up!

The moment was loaded. She held her breath. Her pulse sounded too loud. Oh God, how did he know anyone was watching? In the dimness of the room she couldn't be seen. And he'd been looking straight ahead. It wasn't possible!

The idea came to her that if she thought about him, looked at him, concentrated on him in any way, then he could sense her. Somehow. And so, slowly, incrementally, she began to transfer her focus to the interior of the room instead, her gaze settling on the portrait above the fireplace.

Think of something else...don't look at him...look at the frame, at anything...

A faint gossamer-fine strand of moonlight picked out the aquiline nose of the subject, the somewhat cadaverous features and elongated skull. Deep within her being something was shifting, a veil twitching, a curtain about to be lifted...when the sound of a walking cane on stone broke the trance and she immediately looked out of the window again.

A short pause was all it had been. A nanosecond. But her heart was hammering and she was awash with cold sweat, as now she noticed the long black shape looming over the top of the old man as he stepped into the house.

What the fuck are we dealing with?

Lauren moved away from the gap, allowing the new information to settle.

Were the dark shapes demonic attachments? Did these people bring them in using rituals? How did it happen? And were the ghosts here all victims of that dark magic? Would that be her fate, too?

No one else knows you're here, then? No family?

Just like you

Before she could think further, another guest arrived, this time driving a sports car.

He looked familiar and at first she didn't recognise him, although felt she should. He was small, though - really quite tiny, she thought as he parked the car and began to walk quickly across the courtyard. Was that really him? Couldn't be! But as he drew closer there was little doubt as to his identity. The man was distinctive and famous. She didn't watch television very often but he'd been a news anchor for years and before that a children's TV presenter. He was a household name.

"Sheesh! Even media people!"

The other guests then arrived in rapid succession. Not all were discernible. One was definitely an archbishop. There'd been twelve in total. All male. And all alone. Until the last one. The purr of a powerful elegant car now crunched across the gravel into the courtyard.

A chauffeur held open a rear door and again Lauren stepped back, cloaked by the heavy velvet fabric of the curtains. A hush fell upon the scene that was almost palpable, a shrinking recoil from the living and dead alike. Time fell away, layers peeling back. There was the most horrible heart-clutching moment of anticipation, and transfixed, Lauren watched, unable to stop herself just as had happened at the lake. A woman was swinging her legs demurely to one side, preparing to alight from the car. One black leather glove reached to take the hand of the chauffeur, head dipping, before she stepped out, turned, and stood to face the house. Not the porch entrance. But the house itself and the row of bedroom windows above it.

Rouge spots on alabaster skin…button eyes…a riding crop held high…

Something had changed. The whole atmosphere was charged, the night no longer clear and black. Nor was the wind whipping up and shaking the trees. Instead it was absolutely calm, and thick with fog, the same unearthly sulphuric smog that had formed around the lake and on the moors, the smell of bad drains instantly recognisable. And as she watched, a dozen or more quivering, granular grey forms began to form behind the woman standing in the yard. Others too, were now gravitating towards them en-masse, in a silent, spectral army.

Lauren closed her eyes.

Make it go away. Make it go away. Jesus Christ, please protect me. God and Jesus Christ, please protect me!

A door clicked softly then, and when she opened her eyes the wind had picked up again, the sky had cleared, and the woman was walking into the oak-panelled foyer. Her back was ramrod straight, each step a tight click on the flagstones at the entrance. And towering over her an elongated shadow swept into the house behind, oozing across the walls, instantly darkening the lamp lit entrance.

So they were all here for the ritual sacrifice? Hers! Did they actually summon a diabolical entity, a soulless intelligence, into a host's body? What, for power and money?

Her silent questions settled into the silent hiss of the room.

Footsteps were in the corridor again, doors opening and closing. One thing was for sure, she decided, no way would she spend another night here and live to tell the tale.

So the meeting started at eight o'clock. She pictured the dismal ceremony in the dungeon room she'd seen in the dream. Was it something like that, or worse? And would Hermia do as she said - go and get something to eat and leave her alone to sleep? Could she trust Hermia? The girl had a special ability to soul journey and would probably sense if she attempted to escape.

You can't leave.

And what about Davis?

A single image came then of Hermia handing Davis a

drink of sherry.

Brompton mixture, I think they call it...

And as Lauren tuned into the surprising image in her mind, Hermia looked up and their eyes met - just as they had in her dream on that first night. And this time she knew that Hermia had not seen an empty space. Somehow, on some level, the two of them had connected.

I can't leave Hermia!

A door slammed then, at the far end of the corridor, and in that moment the light in the house dimmed by another degree. There was an overwhelming feeling of being sucked down into a vortex, the same sensation she'd had standing by the lake, when it had been impossible to look away from the horrors trapped within. What happened, she wondered, to those consumed by the darkness? When all the lights of hope went out?

Seized by a terror so deep within herself she could no longer think clearly, Lauren stood motionless by the window, shivering in the thin black dress that stank of wine and garlic, and knew without any doubt whatsoever, that very soon she'd be running for her life.

***

CHAPTER TWENTY-SEVEN

Waiting for eight o'clock seemed interminable, each minute charged, as downstairs the clock struck every quarter of the hour so faintly it could barely be heard. Foggy of mind, she had to strain to listen, to remind herself to concentrate. A single footstep, creak of a floorboard, distant voice or the closing of a door, and the number of chimes counted was lost.

How many rooms did this house have? What about staff? Who was where?

Lying under the covers in the black dress, Lauren watched the door as a cat watches a garden wall, hyper aware of how swiftly and soundlessly Wil could appear out of nowhere. She pushed the dress down from her shoulders in case it opened. God, she was tired. How much of that bloody stuff had they dosed her with?

She thought through the potential scenarios. No doubt they'd assume she was still heavily drugged, and therefore they'd be confident she was secure? Why had Hermia helped her, though? She'd seemed strongly indoctrinated. Then again, they'd connected on another level, a higher one. Or was that just wishful thinking? Could souls contact each other like that, without the physical body?

And had Hermia really given Davis the Brompton Mixture or…?

Her eyelids began to drop.

Then there was another question: if she did manage to get out of here, what about the children at the mill? Would they be in the grounds?

Spike, Badger....no, he's gone now... um, Snout, Puck and I think, Keeper and Watch...

Keeper and Watch?

Maybe they'd been monitoring her all along, and that's why they were snooping around the cottage?

Downstairs in the hall the clock clunked dully, followed by two sharp clangs of the bell. Half past seven? Or only half past six?

She was sinking fast. The effort of being constantly on alert for the slightest sound was taking its toll, and momentarily she slipped dangerously into a semi-dream state. Probably it only lasted a few seconds, but as had happened on the first night at Groom Lake, she once more found herself outside of her body. A preview, as the voice at the lake had said, or a warning?

This time she was standing on the driveway on the far side of the archway, staring down the long dark route leading to the cottage.

I've been here before.

Slowly, dreamily, she then turned to look back at the house. Out of approximately thirty suites none were lit, and there was no sign of life.

"Look sharp!" said a voice next to her ear.

She leapt around.

The drive back to the road was now no longer empty.

Hermia was staring at her. Dressed in the blue mac and flowery wellingtons she projected the same image as that first night, and it occurred to Lauren that the girl had a supernatural ability far more than 'the sight.'

"It's time for you to go. You need to get out of here."

"Who are you? Why did you play innocent?"

"You're not to think of this again, Lauren. You must not remember it. You're being told this so you won't go back for the one you know as Hermia, and risk your own life. That would achieve nothing. Nor must you have her on your mind, hinder, meddle or bind her. Let it all go. I am from a higher dimension."

Lauren nodded.

"Cut her from your mind. Sever the energy channel immediately."

"I don't understand. Why am I here–?"

But Hermia's child image was gradually merging with the scenery, until she'd faded completely.

Lauren jumped awake and for a second or two remained stunned. The room was darkly hushed, the only light a strip beneath the closed door from the lamp lit corridor.

"Fuck, I crashed out!"

Sliding out of bed she scrambled for her shoes, coat and bag, already seeing herself tearing down the drive to the cottage. One chance. One. Please God, it wasn't too late. What time was it? There was no way of knowing. The only option was to just go.

Would anyone be around? A guest who didn't go into the chamber? Considering it unlikely a guest would be excluded, she tiptoed towards the door: whatever they did and whoever they were, it was likely they'd all have to be bound by the same incriminating secrets.

That left Hermia. A heavily programmed child, or one guided by a higher being? Perhaps both? Could she trust her though, or were the dreams tricks of her own mind?

A little preview. Call it a personal gift…

Well, there definitely wasn't any time to think about it.

After pushing a couple of pillows lengthways under the covers and then shrugging on her coat, she crammed the shoes and contents of the bag into the copious hip pockets. The house was heavy in its silence and she stood listening. Think! Options? One was to climb over the balcony, but that would be in full view of the windows opposite and there could be someone there – staff or one of the children? There was the door to the porch and courtyard? That was a main entrance though, and undoubtedly locked. What about a back door?

A horrifying thought came to her, then. She'd completely forgotten - the car was still at Folly Point!

Holy shit!

Her hand closed around the phone in her pocket. Well of course, she'd been drugged into a coma. And still would be if it wasn't for Hermia. She held onto the little piece of plastic. Would there be a signal, though? What if there wasn't? The Moodys? But what could she tell them? And would they help her? What if they knew about what went on here, but chose to turn a blind eye in the name of self-preservation? Or even recruited? What if Glynis had recruited her?

Fuck!

She recalled the shadow following Tyler that day at the cottage. No, the best bet was to run like hell all the way up to Fiddlers Elbow. No time to lose anyway, she'd have to think on her feet.

Each beat of her heart bounced sickeningly as she crept to the door. And then there was how to get to Folly Point for the car. Most of her stuff was still in the boot, so she'd just have to leave the sleeping bag and heater at the cottage, and then hitch a lift from the main road. The plan was coming together, but what about the hooded snoopers at the mill? What if Charon, or one of his minions, saw her? What did they do – bring victims to these people?

With trembling hands she gently pushed down the bedroom door handle and peered into the gloom. The passage was velvety dark, lit faintly by a lamp half way down. Slowly her eyes began to adjust, and then full understanding registered.

Dear God! Please help me!

A row of hooded figures was hanging several feet above the floor all the way along. Monks? Or the deceased brothers of a dark cult? Were they earthbound entities just waiting to latch onto the energy of a living being?

The moment that thought occurred to her, several of them appeared to shift and became aware.

She took a quick breath, softly closing the door behind her.

It was now or never.

Then fled down the corridor in search of the stairs.

***

CHAPTER TWENTY-EIGHT

On reaching the ground floor, Lauren dived into a space underneath the stairwell. A kitchen! There had to be a kitchen, and more than likely it would be here at the back of the house.

All was deathly quiet. Was Davis the only member of staff around or were there others? These were distinguished guests so there'd have to be, surely? From the far end of a corridor, there came a faint clatter of plates and she gravitated towards it. With luck the kitchen door would be open or at least have a key in the lock. It was the best chance, anyway.

Keeping close to the shadows of the wall she darted from room to room, and as she drew closer her stomach groaned with hunger at the aroma of cooking. There were voices too, and she peered around the doorway. A man in a black t-shirt had his back to her, feet up on the table, while a young woman prepared food.

"That old biddy who clicked her fingers and called me, 'Girl!' Honestly, since when did she get off speaking to people like that?"

"Just keep your own counsel, it's best," said the man Lauren now saw had a holster over his shoulder.

"It's my first time here," said the young woman. "I had to sign the Official Secrets Act."

"Yeah."

"I suppose they don't want staff talking to the papers?"

"Won't happen - they own the papers."

"By the way, this might sound daft but have you noticed Judge Landgrave's eyes? When he looks at you?"

"Like a shark?"

"Yeah, weird. Made me go cold all over."

"You seen the guy in the white suit yet? He never speaks, and I mean never."

"God, yes! I handed him a drink earlier and he didn't even look at me."

"Creepy dude. Don't take it personally. I don't think he speaks to any of *them* either. I had a job with the royals a while back and he was the same there."

"What? He didn't speak to the queen?"

The man laughed. "Don't ask me who he is. Like I say, keep your own counsel. Some things are better not known."

She shrugged. "At least it's good money."

"Incredible money."

While they were talking, Lauren scanned the kitchen and noticed a large utility room leading to a stone-walled corridor and an outside door.

The woman was chop-chop-chopping now, concentrating; and the man had plugged himself into his phone and had headphones on. Clearly they felt safe to talk openly, so all the key members, family and guests, must be in the chamber? It was a good time. Briefly, she wondered about Davis and Hermia, but this was probably the only chance there'd be, so without further hesitation Lauren slipped past to the utility room.

Oh, thank God – there's a key in the lock!

She turned it as soundlessly as possible. It made the

faintest of clicks. She held her breath, eased through, and then pulling the door shut behind her, stepped into the night.

It had opened onto a row of facing outhouses and stables, and the faint smell of sweet hay and horse sweat wafted through the ages. For one transitory moment another wave of déjà-vu swept over her, and fear clutched at her heart. A belt of misty rain was blowing across the yard and she lifted her face to the wild freshness of it, grateful to be outside and able to feel the rawness of the elements. Wind was bouncing the branches of firs and pines, whistling off the moors and whipping up leaves in swirls of confetti. Thank God the horrible sulphuric smog had gone and the night was clear again. The woman who'd arrived last, whoever she was, had seemed to bring it with her. Along with a whole legion of other things…

Keeping flush to the wall of the house she moved cautiously now towards the courtyard. On second thoughts it would be far too risky to run over to the archway in full view of the windows. Backtracking, she darted over to the other side of the house, intending to cut across the lawns. There was no time to lose. And for speed, probably better to stay barefoot. With no further thought she then broke into a run.

How many others have run full pelt out across these lawns, pounded the paths in the woods, barefoot and desperate? Don't look back…Just run like hell…

But it was impossible not to. There was someone chasing her. Already! They must have seen her. And silently, stealthily they were closing the gap, catching up fast. Who? More than one? Security guards? Of course! The man with the holster.

Shit!

She was flat out now, sprinting across the grass. The sky was spinning in a kaleidoscope of stars and dizzying treetops, and on reaching the oaks lining the drive she lurched drunkenly towards the nearest one and grabbed a heeled shoe from out of her pocket.

Winging round, gasping for breath, she faced her pursuers. "Stop! Back off–"

But the pursuers were not alive. They weren't chasing her, either.

En-masse, hordes of spectres were gliding like clouds up the drive - gravitating towards the house as if pulled by a powerful magnet. She stared at the unearthly scene. Was this what they were doing in the chamber? Summoning the earthbound dead?

The woman! Was she a satanic witch?

This couldn't be real, it just couldn't be. She had her back to the solidity of the tree, disbelieving what was before her own eyes. No one would accept this should she ever tell the story. And yet it had happened - what she'd seen in the courtyard when the woman arrived earlier, the elongated shadows attached to people, the hanging hooded figures in the upstairs corridor - all of it was true.

I'm drugged. It could be a trick of the mind.

But she hadn't been drugged when Tyler came to fix the boiler, nor when she'd gone to the lake…

No, it's because of the drugs. They're hallucinatory. And I've been depressed and that can cause psychosis. It's all explainable.

The sinister entities, hundreds of them now, were blending into the fabric of the house, and black goo began to slide over the stones. As she'd done at the lake, she took her focus off the house so that it was only on the edge of her vision, and as exactly as before, the whole building subsequently became a void. It quite simply vanished, became uncreated, sucking everything around it into a black hole.

Was that what this was then – creation versus anti-creation - the destruction of life itself? Were the people who let this demonic intelligence in, for personal gain, unaware of the enormity of what they'd done until it was too late? The horror of what anti-Christ could actually mean sank like a weighted stone: the anti-Christ not being one evil person, but a multitude of soulless entities that needed the lowest vibration of fear to enter our dimension.

And attach to, or inhabit, human hosts?

At that moment she suddenly became aware of a tug beneath the earth, a strong pulling sensation that rooted her feet as it had at the lake. And the air was crackling with the ominous static of an imminent storm. The longer she lingered, she realised, watching the scene, the more it was drawing her into its drama.

Come on, move!

She had a chance. She could make it. Turning to face the drive, she ran along the line of trees towards the cottage, ignoring sharp stabs from stones or twigs, the only sound the bang of her heart beat and the drumming of her feet.

All along I knew...was warned...wouldn't listen...couldn't believe or accept...Why the hell didn't I leave on that first night? Why?

More and more shades were emerging from the forest, but she knew now not to look. Fear made it worse. Like attracted like and the more fear you had the more you got. Focusing on the horror gave it life. Too late, she kept thinking. She'd learned too late. But why had she refused to take heed of all the warnings and been so determined to see the lake, to stay here, to let Wil Landgrave lead her into the house? Curiosity? Or something deeper?

The drive was far longer than she remembered and fatigue was setting into her limbs, the poison they'd given her twisting and burning her lungs, crashing a gong in her head. But despite the pain she speeded up. There was a horrible groaning noise like an old rusty ship capsizing and the ground was turning black. She wasn't going to make it after all, would be consumed in the same dark vortex as the others - hundreds of them, maybe thousands, trapped for all eternity in a low vibration they could never escape. Was that what hell was?

Her heart was about to give out. She could run no more, was about to fall to the ground. Would be stuck...drawn in...overpowered...When a sudden dramatic dip in temperature and a blast of icy air blew straight through her.

The ghostly apparitions, she realised, were rushing past. The tide of energy was surging towards the house, not her. They were not on her timeline. Or even in her dimension. And with that knowledge her optimism was vigorously renewed. Clingbine Cottage was now within reach and she gave it one last push to get there, finally and gratefully lunging for the ash tree next to where her car should be.

Oh dear God, she felt sick. The ground was rolling in an ocean swell and her stomach squeezed tight as a fist.

Did anyone tell her it was human flesh?

A plate full of squishy morsels in grey sauce flashed before her and she doubled over, retching repeatedly until acid scorched her throat, tears streamed, and she was on her hands and knees with a head that clanged like a discordant orchestra.

I have to get back up. I have to…

Her own small hands splaying on the earth suddenly seemed alien, too white in the light of the moon, and this time the feeling of déjà-vu stayed longer than previously, dancing on the periphery of her memory.

A familiar laughter ricocheted through the trees.

I know now…something… what? What was it?

As soon as the memory had registered, however, it disappeared again. But there'd been something…Something so important…

There was no time to think about it though, and she forced herself onwards, scrabbling for the key to the door.

There was precious little in the cottage that couldn't be left behind. Good thing or not a good thing, she wondered, fretting about the car and all its contents. Not much choice, though, and there wasn't much time to get herself together. Quickly she downed a glass of tap water, grimaced at the taste, flew into the bathroom, changed back into the clothes she'd discarded from the walk up to the hill, then crammed everything else into the holdall. At least she had something to her name, she thought, stuffing a couple of leftover biscuits into her mouth, even if it was little more than a change of clothes. It would be better to be destitute than risk coming back here.

Standing at the door five minutes later, she zipped up the waterproof. Okay, what next? Moodys or the main road? Which? And pray to God none of those snoops from the mill were around. Did they know what had happened to her these past few days? Were they on the pay roll? Would it be their turn next if they didn't do what they were told?

Before venturing into the night, with her hand on the door, she closed her eyes. "God, please grant me the courage I need. Please, my angels and guides, please help me!"

About to open the door, she suddenly remembered Hannah and pulled out her phone. There'd be a signal once she got clear of the ford and onto higher ground. The mobile phone lit up and one bar of connection flickered then failed. She tapped out the text and pressed 'Send.' It didn't, instead remaining in the sending process. Okay, well hopefully the text would go as soon as a signal reappeared.

Opening the door she picked up the holdall, still deliberating which way to go. The main road beyond Fiddlers Rest would probably be best, although it was bleak and deserted, and if anyone came searching for her she'd stand out like a Belisha Beacon.

The Moodys, then?

But could she trust Tyler? Would he help her?

I think I'll report it to the police, as well.

Oh no, you don't want to do that

No, the long haul up to the main road it would have to be. She dropped the phone into her pocket and turned to close the door behind her.

"Evening!"

She swung round. A man stood before her, dressed in a hoodie and black jeans, and she saw the resemblance at once. Close up he could be Tyler Moody's son.

***

Chapter Twenty-Nine

Charon was standing well back from the doorway, his face partly shrouded by a hood. Behind him the crescendo of wind rushing through the forest was escalating, a low pan pipe howling down the hills.

Her heart plunged like a brick down a well. Oh God, this was it! He'd been sent to deal with her, hadn't he? She wouldn't stand a chance.

But how did he know she'd gone? Or did he and his scouts – Watch, Keeper, Snout et al - have permanent instructions to guard the estate? No one could do it more surreptitiously, that was for sure. Just how long had this man been keeping tabs on her?

She kept her eyes and voice steady. So far he hadn't moved towards her or attempted to block the way. "We haven't met. Do I know you?"

Charon's eyes glinted beneath thick black eyebrows. Close up he was handsome in a way that Tyler was not, with eyes that slanted upwards at the outer corners, his cheekbones more pronounced. The expression he wore, though, was identical. Both carried the same hunt-or-be-hunted energy of a wild animal, a starving forager constantly vigilant. There was a sense of him being on the very edge of life, that nothing would ever surprise him, and that all he had to do was as his namesake suggested - take the money and facilitate the passage.

From light to dark, sane to insane…

She saw him as she once had in dream state, sitting night after night in the old mill with its broken glass, dripping cellar, and draughty floorboards. The sound of children crying themselves to sleep echoed in his mind every bit as much as the ghoulish whistling down the chimney, and the scratching of branches on the windows. Out of the corner of his eye, she guessed he saw grey shapes flit across the fire-glow of the walls, and shadows creep across a stairwell stained with damp. Once, his oil lamp had snuffed out for no reason and something had hissed his name. His heart had clenched in fear. There was no way out for Charon, she thought. He was every bit as trapped as the entities rising out of the lake.

"Saw you the other day," he said. "You walked past. Don't you remember?"

"Oh yes, of course. My name's Lauren," she said, hauling the bag onto her shoulder. "And you?"

"Charon."

She dropped the key into her pocket and felt for the phone, feigning naivety. "I'm just off out."

"So I see. Bit late for a hike, isn't it?"

Keeping distance between them, she stepped to one side and backed onto the open driveway, trying not to think about a possible attack. If he even attempted to grab her it was game over: she'd run but he'd be whippet fast and possibly there were others around she couldn't see. Besides, there was a chance he didn't know she'd been captive at the house. She latched onto that. Maybe, just maybe… he didn't know she'd been there?

The first words that came into her mouth flew out.

"Actually, I went to a restaurant the other night, had too much to drink and left my car there. I've got to go and get it."

He regarded her as steadily as a hunter eyeing its prey. "Bit late," he repeated.

She really did not owe him an explanation, but he was only a lunge away, and that all-important barrier between them could not be breached. It was imperative.

Keeping her tone light, pretending for all her worth that nothing unusual was going on, she said, "I know. Embarrassing really, but I only just woke up and now I can't rest knowing it's still up there. It could get nicked or broken into, even an old heap like mine."

"Might be able to help you there. That's why I came round, isn't it?"

A fine spray of rain blew against her face. That was why he came? How the hell did he know about her car?

"Oh?"

"I've got your car. Friend of mine contacted me and we thought it might be yours." He gestured towards the mill. "It's over at my place if you want to come and get it."

It was all over, wasn't it?

Her voice came from so far away it no longer sounded like her own. "What? Sorry? A friend thought it was mine? What friend? I don't understand."

"My uncle Ty. We're looking out for you, see?"

"Looking out for me?"

She must have looked as dumb as she felt, because his shoulders suddenly slumped and he shook his head. "Fuck knows we tried hard enough to make you leave. Look, move into the shade all right? We're in the middle of the drive here. Got your car keys, have you?"

Her hands were shaking noticeably as he took hold of her elbow and manoeuvred her into the shadow of the cottage.

She clutched the key in her pocket, pushing the sharp metal into her palm. "Yes."

His voice was soft and low. "You're going to have to get the hell out of here. Fucking Glynis, that stupid mare, should never in a million years have got anyone here, especially a lass on her own."

Was this a trick? Through the sickly, drugged pulsating thud of her head, she looked past him towards the lane. It was a long way up to Fiddlers Elbow. Running from him wasn't an option, especially feeling like this. And besides, if he had her car and Tyler and he were related, what choice was there?

"You've been up at the house, haven't you?"

She nodded. "I went out to dinner with Wil Landgrave."

"I know. Look, just get the hell away from Groom Lake, will you? We tried to scare you out, but Glynis said you started kicking off about the police. One more week and you'd have been all right but then you went out with Landgrave."

She listened, stunned. What he was saying was the opposite to what she'd thought, and she struggled to compute the new information. What? So he and Tyler could be trusted after all? No, this was a trick. Yet something did ring true…something that stirred deep inside.

"To be honest, when we knew you were up at the Grange we didn't expect you to leave again. We know you know what this is, Lauren. No point playing innocent. In fact, playing anymore games could get us both killed."

She nodded.

"Nobody gets to leave here. And they make sure you won't have any kind of a life if you try. We decided to look out for you, that's all."

"Why?"

He smiled tightly, continually checking the drive to the house. "Look, I'm taking a huge risk here. Ty was told to pick up your car. We sell it on for scrap and keep the money. We didn't expect you'd get out of there again after you'd been so fucking stupid. Anyway, miracles of miracles, looks like we've got one last chance. You must have an angel looking after you for it to happen twice."

She barely heard him. There was too much to take in. Still in shock, shaking from head to foot – from cold, hunger, drug withdrawal or fear, she couldn't be sure – Lauren nodded and he let go of her elbow.

"Follow me, all right? Be very quick and don't speak."

She had to jog to keep up. The lane, as before, was awash: the bordering woods a hush of icy darkness trickling with invisible streams. And this time the raw wind on her face was welcome, helping off-set the drowsy effect of the sedatives. As she hurried after him, the ke-wick, ke-wick, ke-wick of a tawny owl from a nearby hillside pierced the night air and momentarily her spirits soared. Life. There was life not too far away, and with every step further away from Groom Lake the oppression began to lift, and the journey onwards became clearer.

She held tightly onto the phone in her pocket.

I have to get to Hannah.

On reaching the mill, Charon shot over to the side gate where she'd first seen him, and ushered her through to the yard at the back. "Car's in the lock-up. Should be getting crushed tomorrow - same bloke who fixed your windscreen. And the bump. Careless that, Lauren."

The bright friendly garage came to mind, with its coffee machine, radio blaring and orange chairs; together with the smiling face of the owner and the cheery mechanic who apparently also crushed stolen cars. She nearly smiled, already thanking him as they scooted across the yard, when her attention was drawn to a row of ashen faces looking down from the attic window. Possessed of vacant expressions, some clawed at the glass and one lifted a hand to wave.

Charon had unlocked the outbuilding when she stopped, and he glanced up to where she was looking. "You can see them?"

"The ghosts?"

The incline of his head was so slight she almost missed it.

"I never saw anything until I came here. But yes, I can see faces at the window. I could the other day, too. But Hermia said there were other children here – funny names – Spike, Snout, Watch, Keeper... So are they alive or ghosts?"

He didn't answer.

"What happened to Badger?"

"I wouldn't know about that, Lauren."

"What they're doing up at the house? It's Satanism." Still he said nothing.

She dropped her voice to barely a whisper. "These are people at the very top - government and household names."

His dark eyes held hers. "Sometimes it's too late for them, Lauren. People think it's the in-crowd, a club, a game–"

The memory of the man in the robe descending into a black chamber, of the echoing words in his head as he recited a ritual he suddenly, horribly, understood, flashed before her.

"Until it's not anymore? And they realise what they signed up to?"

"Exactly. And then it's far, far too late."

"I wonder what happens when they get past a certain level? After that they must be in a special kind of hell, so far beyond the–"

"Actually some of them don't give a shit from day one. Come on, concentrate. Right, this car is officially scrapped as from tomorrow morning first light. So no one's going to be looking for it. I haven't seen you and if I have you're dealt with, ok? So don't go up to see Glynis, and don't do anything stupid like speeding or trying to sell it for a long, long time. I've taken a fucking shed load of risks for you. Now get going."

Following him into the old barn she prayed he wouldn't change his mind. "So why are you?"

"Call it karma."

She walked with him to the car. "Why don't you leave? What's in it for you here? You can't like what they make you do?"

"Got to keep watch."

They were less than a foot apart in a breezy lock-up awhirl with leaves. Wind whistled through the doors.

"How do you mean?"

"On the family. The Moody family's always been here - millers, blacksmiths, publicans, farmers." He glanced over in the direction of The Grange. "Something went wrong.

Maybe one of them sold out for money – but that monstrosity of a house was built over a cave with a sacred well. And where the pines are? That used to be a druids' forest, a lush dell full of life."

She found she could see it. Could envision the white robed people by the river and the golden hue of the valley…How had she dreamt all of this? How? And why? There was so much that was vague, dreams merging with other times and dimensions.

"Why are you lingering, Woman? You need to get going."

Holding onto the car door, she looked into his eyes. So he saw the ghosts and lived with centuries of ancestral karma, as he called it. Maybe he guarded the souls of the family that had, at some point long ago, sold out their own kind?

"You need to go," he repeated.

"What about Hermia? I can't just abandon her." She looked in the direction of the house. "You have no idea what's–"

"Lauren!"

She turned back to face him.

"I don't know a Hermia," he said.

"The girl – about twelve years old, really pale, wears flowery wellies and–"

He was shaking his head. "I know every last kid that goes in there and there is no Hermia."
"She looked after me. Sat on my bed. Told me about the ceremony and…"

He was still shaking his head. And when he spoke it was in such a grave tone there was no mistaking the authenticity. "The only Hermia I ever heard of was a little girl who would have been the same age as you and me if she'd lived."

Her mouth dropped open.

But there was no time to let the information register properly. They'd each sensed it at the same time, even before a small figure materialised out of nowhere at the door. Both turned towards a boy in his early teens by the look of it. Dressed in a hoodie, he jerked a thumb in the direction of Groom Lake.

Something had happened at the house.

***

CHAPTER THIRTY

"Go, before I change my mind."

"What's happened? Do they know I've gone? How?"

"Just go. Now!"

"Thank you with all my heart and soul," Lauren said, jumping into the car.

Without another word she then reversed out and exited Groom Lake at speed. No chance to think anything through, plan ahead, or even comprehend what had just happened or why. All that mattered was survival. Her knuckles were bone shiny as she gripped the steering wheel. The night was black as pitch, the wet lane a tunnel of trees, and the canopy overhead cracked and swayed in the wind. Firs shivered either side, sheltering the lane from the roar of cross winds, until finally she reached open moorland and a blast of fresh night air buffered the car.

There's no Hermia. She's not alive.

At Fiddlers Elbow she automatically turned right onto the straight moorland road towards Owlbury, foot flat to the board. And it was only after ten minutes, when the glaring lights of town bobbed on the horizon, that the question occurred to her - why on earth had she come this way? The other exit from Groom Lake led back to the A49, whereas Owlbury was a town with only one way out; and that was across the river into the mountains. A dead end.

Hermia's not alive.

Levelling with the forty mile per hour zone, she took her foot off the gas as the conversation with Charon slowly began to filter back in.

But Hermia had been so real. And they'd seemed to know each other. There'd been a recognition between them, a purpose, right from the very first night in the dream. Then there was the same way they'd both lapsed into a trance, had paralysis, and dream-like speech and actions. There were also the moments of profound déjà-vu she'd experienced ever since arriving...and the effect the woman with the riding crop had on her...

It almost made sense and yet it didn't.

So what had happened at the house? Were they after her? The boy – Watch or Keeper – hadn't even needed to speak before Charon had physically bundled her into the car, and it occurred to her again to wonder why he and Tyler had risked so much to help her. Why they cared?

A little girl who would have been about the same age as you and me had she lived.

A roundabout was looming up far too fast, and startled she slammed on the brakes. Bloody hell, she must have blanked out! If it was noticed she'd gone missing they could easily send someone to track her down, and an accident was the last thing she needed. What if the Landgraves controlled the police? Recalling the Moodys' aversion to calling them she now saw that situation in a markedly different light. And picturing an officer bundling her into the back of a patrol car, she pulled into a side street, just as her phone sparked into life with the buzz of a text.

It was from Hannah.

Switching off the engine she re-read the neon bright

message. Oh yes, of course – it was a reply to the one she'd sent just before Charon turned up. A lifetime had passed since then.

Oh, thank God! Hannah…

'What on earth's happened? I can come and get you, yes. Heading out now. Where are you exactly?'

***

CHAPTER THIRTY-ONE

Hannah hadn't seemed surprised. In fact, as they sat in Hannah's living room by the fire, it was clear by the way her steady grey eyes regarded her that she'd been expecting this, or at least something like it.

"Do you want another hot chocolate?"

Lauren shook her head. "No, thanks. My stomach's really sensitive."

"I'm not surprised. Brompton Mixture, you said? Isn't that a cocktail of heroin and chloroform among other things? And the child told you that? There was a child administering it?"

Lauren nodded. How could she tell her that Hermia was a ghost? Hannah would surely think the whole thing was a hallucination? And it could have been, had it not been for the fact Charon had also known a girl by that name, one who would have been the same age 'had she lived'.

"Another slice of toast?"

"No, honestly. But, thank you."

What she really wanted to do was sleep for at least a month, but even with the car in Hannah's garage it wasn't safe to hang around.

She looked at the clock. "It's getting late. I ought to find a hotel or get on the road–"

"That would be absolutely crazy and I won't hear of it. No, you can have the spare room with pleasure. We'll catch up properly tomorrow - you're exhausted and you need to rest."

"Thank you, but to be honest I'm not relaxed enough to sleep."

Wide-eyed and shivering despite the heating on full and a roaring fire, she got the distinct impression Hannah was waiting for her to say something else. But what?

"Don't you find it odd we met up again after all these years, in a place like this - miles from anywhere?" Hannah said. "I mean, what are the chances?"

Lauren struggled to formulate her thoughts. "I know. And I've got the strongest feeling I'm personally connected to Groom Lake in some way, but I don't know how. It was extremely strange right from the start, but then you knew that – you warned me about the area."

She began to relate the disorientating out of body dreams and the experience at the lake, touching on how she'd seen ghosts for the first time in her life. She told her about Nine Rings Hill and the line of hooded figures vanishing over the edge, and the ashen faces of children at the windows of the mill, only stopping short when it came to the man descending into a dungeon for what she realised now was possibly a black mass. For some reason that felt like a step too far, and not for the first time she wondered how she could possibly have dreamt about that? It was like being given more and more pieces of a jigsaw yet still not being able to see the picture.

But Hannah was unperturbed. "Go on!"

Glossing over the dark ritual she'd witnessed through the man's eyes, she went on to describe the way she'd met

Wil Landgrave and how she'd ended up at the house drugged, omitting the hallucinatory rape scenes, which had all been in dream state, and also the incubus and the premonitions. Those bits were still too raw, too deeply personal and shaming.

"I think he must have spiked my drink twice - at the pub and again at the restaurant."

Hannah nodded.

"Why are you here though, do you mind me asking?" said Lauren. "You don't seem shocked by anything I've just told you, that's all."

There was a flicker of indecision, barely discernible, before Hannah answered. "I don't think anything can surprise me ever again, Lauren. But what about you?"

"How do you mean?"

"You now know there's evil and black magic on this earth, that it's real, it works, and is used?"

"Yes."

"And black magic only works through artful deception, the gateway being our weaknesses?"

Lauren nodded. 'Sometimes too painful to even confess to', she wanted to add.

"All right then, I'll tell you something. I've been trying to find out what happened to Geoff, my husband. It was after he came here...."

It was a blessed relief not to have to think any more, not to have to try and work it all out: the man in the white suit who never spoke, the ghost of Hermia, the bizarre dreams that merged with reality, the hypnotic trance at the lake, and how she'd been tricked and lured almost to her death. Now she was out of immediate physical danger it was difficult to believe she'd stayed there at all, and yet at the time each step of the way had felt like a compulsion, almost as if predestined.

I mean, no one else knows you're here, then? No family–

"...Geoff was a surgeon when he joined what I'm going to call the dark cult. It was a kind of all-boys thing if you like, with drinks, charity dinners, and weekends away for things like mountain climbing and outdoor bound stuff. The details of what they did was vague, to be honest, and he wouldn't tell me what they did at the lodges. I found the regalia once, in a box on top of the wardrobe – a long black gown with a hood, and a leather-bound ceremonial book. When I asked him about it he said it was nothing, just symbolic play-acting and that I shouldn't have been snooping around in matters to do with the 'brotherhood'. He was furious, and really turned on me..."

Lauren found herself losing entire chunks of the conversation as she continually jumped the gun: in some strange way she knew what was coming...knew and yet didn't.

"I saw him less and less. And I never liked where it was going. Had a bad feeling. Where we'd once been close a great chasm opened up between us. He'd be out maybe three nights a week with the dark cult, and on top of that he was doing a huge amount of private surgery. He got a lot of extra work, moving rapidly through the ranks. There was a partnership in a London clinic, he bought a nursing home, sat on various committees, and travelled the world giving lucrative talks. He did far more private work than the public job he was paid to do. In fact, I found out later he was increasingly late for ward rounds and clinics. Didn't care, either! And that was the thing, because it was a complete anathema - he'd always been so fastidious, you see?"

Hannah's face was fading in and out.

"Do you want some water, Lauren? Honestly, I think you ought to get some sleep."

"I can't. There's something bugging me. Your husband… Geoff…You said you came here trying to find out what happened to him, but didn't you say you were divorced, not widowed?"

She nodded. "Oh yes, we divorced all right. But then I heard he'd gone missing. He hadn't turned up for clinic four days on the trot, and I think even his senior reg. had had enough. Turned out I'd been blamed for breaking his heart - you should have seen the looks when I went to the hospital to speak to his colleagues. Boy had they made up their minds! But what they didn't know was that by then he didn't have a heart. No moral compass. He'd just fabricated a story about me and people believed him, largely because of his status and, of course, because of how he used to be. Easy, eh? But he'd changed and that's what they couldn't have known. Something had happened to him and it happened after he joined what I will only ever refer to as the dark cult."

"And so why–?"

"What led me here to Owlbury? Okay, well what few people knew was that Geoff was a master of ceremonies, and that's why he was travelling all over the world as it turned out, to attend particular lodges. The higher up in the dark cult they go, the more exacting the trials, and the more terrible the secret, you see? And there are very few at the top. Globally. What binds them together is horrific. So, by then they trust and venerate each other far more than the people they're supposed to love, let alone serve from a position of trust. Because when they reach that point they can't do anything else."

Sometimes it's too late, Lauren. People think it's a game until it's not a game anymore.

"Lodges? There's a huge white temple in the grounds behind D'Avranches Grange."

"Yes."

"And you believe Geoff went there?"

"Definitely. Because that's where the top brass go to do the final rite. The worst one. And Geoff was in line to be initiated into the final chamber."

Chamber...

"I found all this out from one of his colleagues, or brothers in arms, who was getting nervous. He told me Geoff would be hanged and his eyes cut out if he tried to leave. Not only that but he'd be hunted down on the other side of the veil, too – persecuted eternally. And believe me the punishment of the soul is far worse than anything they could do to you here on earth."

"What does that mean?"

"They keep them in extreme fear of what they call the watchers after death. He had a particular terror, apparently, of what he said was a man in a white suit, something I never understood or got to the bottom of."

"Oh my God – he wasn't alive! So that's why he never spoke!"

Hannah frowned. "Geoff had a breakdown in the end. He'd told this colleague, who obviously has to remain nameless, that he felt watched all the time, that shadows crept around his room at night and followed him down the street - things like that. He'd put the blame on me to avert others from discovering the real reason for his depressive and increasingly erratic state. So possibly he'd had a change of mind, or maybe got scared and didn't want to go through with it. He'd told one person, you see - confided in this colleague who was a member of the same cult. He still is, of course, but he wasn't flying as close to the sun. Maybe he was a little less dedicated, ambitious, or greedy? Geoff was going to be appointed as head of a global medical organisation, one that dictates to world governments."

"That was his reward?"

"Yes. Untold wealth and erm…other things…"

The memory of men in black hooded robes vanishing off the side of the mountain floated into Lauren's mind, along with the dream of the one who'd faltered in his ceremonial address. Was that Hannah's husband? And was this final rite Geoff had baulked at, the one happening again at D'Avranches Grange tomorrow night? The one for which she was the intended sacrifice?

"But he wouldn't go through with the last ritual?"

"His colleague thinks that's most likely the case.

"And that ritual is always at D'Avranches Grange?"

Now the images came thick and fast, from the hanging corpse with the empty eye sockets to the dreams of the cold, dripping underground chamber that Charon said was built over a sacred well.

"But why me?"

Hannah shook her head. "Sorry?"

"No, no…nothing. So what does the last ritual involve? The one he couldn't do?"

"Apparently they have to kill someone. The person has to be pure as in a good person with morals and a soul. The victim must be terrified first, with torture, and then the adrenalin fuelled blood drained and drunk. I can only think that was the point Geoff realised his soul was about to be sold."

The effect was akin to a jug of icy water poured down the spine. And it felt, for a moment, as if the ground beneath her had opened up, and that she would fall through it and never stop falling.

Hermia's face swam before her.

She, Lauren, had been saved.

By a ghost.

"I know her…"

"Who?"

"But why did they save me? Charon and Tyler? And who was Hermia?"

"You need to sleep, Lauren. Come on, lean on me."

"My whole life has flipped. I feel like I'm going insane. And why are you here at the same time as me? I don't understand. There's something missing."

The last words she remembered were, "Possibly because you're too enmeshed. Part of it, you see…?"

***

Chapter Thirty-Two

When Lauren awoke, it was to the misty rays of morning. The bedroom had been decorated blandly for successive tenants, the walls off-white and the carpet brown nylon. But the comforting aroma of a log fire downstairs, and toast and coffee filled the house.

She lay still. All was quiet, the clock showing it was ten in the morning. It took a minute to register. Ten o'clock! She leapt up. That was twelve hours of totally dreamless sleep! And how different the world looked, she thought, when you'd slept.

"Would you be receptive to a healing session?" Hannah asked later, as they sat in the lounge with fresh cups of coffee between them. "Only if you want. Just to clear some of the energies. I don't take offence, it's entirely up to you."

"How does that work?"

They chatted for a long time, however, before Hannah asked her the question that finally began to make sense of the jigsaw. And the picture that emerged was not a comfortable one, not expected, and came as an enormous, life-changing…no, more than life-changing…soul changing, shock.

"When I knew you as a student nurse, you said you lived with an aunt. Was it Auntie Claire? It's coming back to me now."

A tiny knot stirred and tightened deep inside. "That's right."

Hannah looked thoughtful for a while, before saying, "You mentioned that Hermia knew you had no relatives?"

Just like you…

"Mmm."

"Sorry, not meaning to pry."

"It's ok."

What was coming? She began to psyche herself up.

"I was just wondering if you had, you know, someone to go to?"

"No, Auntie Claire died over a year ago. She brought me up, although I can't remember anything before about the age of seven. We had this wonderful holiday on the South Wales coast, the Gower, after…after…"

A memory snapped into place then, as firmly as a cog clicking into a wheel. And locked. Of a damp cottage with fields either side of a long tree-lined track…the smell of mould… and… No! There had been no other holiday.

"Ah, I'm so sorry to hear…"

Hannah's voice trailed away.

"Robin's Nest," she heard her own voice say. "That was where I came from. Auntie Claire told me she'd collected me from Robin's Nest, and I always thought it was just a sweet way of saying she'd adopted me, you know like some people say they got the baby from a stork? But now–"

Hannah had been nodding, but suddenly her face blanched. "Oh, my good god!"

"What? What is it?"

"Lauren, Lord Landgrave fosters children from the Robin's Nest Children's Home in Shrewsbury."

The missing piece!

The shock was so profound she flailed around for something to hold onto. Not all of those dreams had been dreams. They were memories!

You must have an angel looking after you for it to happen twice.

"Maybe Auntie Claire came looking for her niece after your parents died?

"She'd been in the Navy."

"Is it possible they didn't know an aunt would come looking? Is it possible you had to be sent back to Robin's Nest, and that the family was forced to let you go?"

"Hermia!" She could see her now: standing at the upper floor window of the Grange, her hand held up to wave, ashen-faced, as Lauren walked down the drive next to a boy with dark hair - one who escorted her to a cottage by a five bar gate to wait for a taxi. "Oh, God! Charon said... oh, God. She died and I lived!"

"But what could you have done? Age six or seven, was it?"

"She was a ghost, not real. They must have killed her–"

"So you escaped physically, but you also carried a burden, a guilt that blighted your life. Maybe you had to come back in order to find the truth? And Hermia helped you."

"But she seemed to believe everything, that the play as she called it, was a good thing."

"Mind controlled," said Hannah.

"Yes."

"But that's not the soul. Her higher self was helping you, that's the thing."

"She couldn't remote view the chamber, the dungeon. She didn't know about the torture and the murder, did she? She didn't fully understand the evil."

"Maybe she wasn't supposed to? It could have been too

horrific. And it's likely her soul departed long before the murder took place. That's just a theory."

Lauren considered Hannah's husband and his fear of the man in the white suit, and of being trapped after death like all the others in the woods and the lake. Didn't they know it wasn't real anymore, that their souls could fly free?

"How did Tyler and Charon know me? I remember now the way Tyler stared on that first day. It was like he'd had an electric shock. How did they know? Twenty years on?"

Hannah shrugged. "Well, you're very distinctive to look at, with your white blonde hair and those aqua eyes, so fine boned, so pale…and so, so nervous. And when anyone goes through something as traumatic as that, they'll bond at soul level. Maybe it was one of those things - they just knew?"

"But how come I went back there? Of all the places to choose for a holiday?"

"You said your life wasn't going well? That you were in yet another relationship where you felt unequal and unworthy, and you thought that's all you deserved?"

She nodded. "A bloody lifelong pattern. Must have 'gullible fool' stamped on my forehead."

"Or trauma bonded child."

Lauren began to wring her hands. "I'm struggling to take all of this in, to accept it."

"Yes."

"Yet it makes sense of my whole life."

"And you came through it. You can see what happened and that none of it was your fault. You survived what most would not."

"And you? The link…"

Hannah shook her head, staring into the log fire. "We

don't know how all the quantum entanglements work, the universe, the true nature of our existence, do we? All I know is that for some reason I was the one who was here for you at this particular time, as Hermia was in spirit. And that you've helped me solve a few more pieces of my own puzzle. I can tell you this - I remember very clearly from our nursing days that you were the only one who was kind. The rest bitched because I was just that little bit different. But you were kind. I remember your eyes, lagoon blue. You reminded me of a mermaid. Maybe it's all predestined, I honestly don't know. But how long can we keep writing things off as coincidence before it becomes mathematically impossible?"

"Hmmm..." Lauren prevaricated for a minute, and then decided she ought to tell Hannah about the vision after all – the one of the man who'd suddenly had enlightenment, an illumination of the soul. Maybe it would help answer Hannah's final questions?

After she'd finished, neither of them spoke for a while.

"I'm so sorry about your husband, Hannah."

"All of this was meant to happen for me too, you know? I've been in limbo for a long time, never really knowing what went on. And now I'm free."

"Thank you, Hannah. I haven't actually said that yet, so thank you."

"Thank you, too. For being kind to me when I had no friends at that hospital, which I found doubly hard because of the energies there, by the way. That building was heavy with the earthbound dead, believe me. And for sharing with me the vision of the man in the underground chamber. I feel in my heart of hearts that it was Geoff, which sets me free, because now I know he connected with the Divine again before it was too late. So thank you. I did love him once, you know."

"Do you think the dark cult will ever face the consequences of what they're doing? That any of them will, including all those complicit, who know but do nothing?"

"Of course. Maybe not in this life, but absolutely in the next. Their choice."

Lauren saw the man in the white suit then, floating into her mind's eye. "I wonder who he is, the man in the white suit?"

"I wouldn't think about him."

Startled, she glanced up to find Hannah's steady grey eyes fixed on her.

"I was told Geoff saw the man in the white suit at every single event he attended, including in the bathroom mirror, as did most of the others. If you think about him he'll materialise."

"Fuck!"

"He can't touch you. Know that! He needs fear to exist, that's the thing."

"All a trick."

"Exactly. It's all a trick. An illusion. All in the mind."

"Which the dark cult know, but most people don't."

"Exactly."

They both fell into silent contemplation for a long time, until the fire began to die back to glowing embers and a fresh sheet of rain spattered across the windows.

"So," Lauren said eventually. "I can't honestly say where I go from here, Hannah. I have absolutely no idea what to do."

"Maybe start with not panicking and doing nothing? Just, for now, be in the moment. Acknowledge the enormity of what you've come through."

"I should probably consider therapy or–"

"If that's right for you. But you know this is spiritual, at the core that's what it is."

She nodded. "And so much bigger than just me. My God, Hannah, what they do!"

"I know. And they've recruited the world's most powerful people. Perhaps we're not powerless, though? Have you thought about that? Maybe all we have to do is hold the light."

"How?"

"Picture it. Be it. Act always as you would if the other person was yourself. Mostly that's what you'll get back and it will expand. If you don't, walk away because it's not good enough."

"I've got to be practical though. There are realities to face."

"Well, I've got an empty house in The Lakes, and I'm lonely. Looking back, I always have been. Perhaps you could help me by using a spare room until you're back on your feet?"

Lauren smiled and was about to say she couldn't possibly impose and would have to pay the going rate, and wouldn't stay long, when Hannah added, "No guilt, no stress, and no pressure to move on…"

The fish hook inside tugged a little, and then loosened its grip.

Go with it, Lauren. All will be well…just go with it…

And this time she listened to her own voice. "Thank you," she said. "I'd appreciate that enormously."

***

REFERENCES

'The Nag Hammadi Gnostic Gospels'
'On the Mechanics of Consciousness' by Ishtar Bentov
'The Committee of 300' by Dr John Coleman
'Bloodlines of the Illuminati' by F. Springmeier
'The Celestine Prophecy' by James Redfield

MORE BOOKS BY SARAH ENGLAND

FATHER OF LIES
A DARKLY DISTURBING OCCULT HORROR TRILOGY: BOOK 1

Ruby is the most violently disturbed patient ever admitted to Drummersgate Asylum, high on the bleak moors of northern England. With no improvement after two years, Dr Jack McGowan finally decides to take a risk and hypnotises her. With terrifying consequences.
A horrific dark force is now unleashed on the entire medical team, as each in turn attempts to unlock Ruby's shocking and sinister past. Who is this girl? And how did she manage to survive such unimaginable evil? Set in a desolate ex-mining village, where secrets are tightly kept and intruders hounded out, their questions soon lead to a haunted mill, the heart of darkness...and the Father of Lies.

***

TANNERS DELL - BOOK 2

Now only one of the original team remains – Ward Sister Becky. However, despite her fiancé, Callum, being unconscious and many of her colleagues either dead or critically ill, she is determined to rescue Ruby's twelve-year-old daughter from a similar fate to her mother.

But no one asking questions in the desolate ex-mining village Ruby hails from ever comes to a good end. And as the diabolical history of the area is gradually revealed, it seems the evil invoked is both real and contagious.

Don't turn the lights out yet!

***

MAGDA – BOOK 3

The dark and twisted community of Woodsend harbours a terrible secret – one tracing back to the age of the Elizabethan witch hunts, when many innocent women were persecuted and hanged.

But there is a far deeper vein of horror running through this village, an evil that once invoked has no intention of relinquishing its grip on the modern world. Rather, it watches and waits with focused intelligence, leaving Ward Sister Becky and CID Officer Toby constantly checking over their shoulders and jumping at shadows.

Just who invited in this malevolent presence? And is the demonic woman who possessed Magda back in the sixteenth century the same one now gazing at Becky whenever she looks in the mirror?

Are you ready to meet Magda in this final instalment of the trilogy? Are you sure?

***

The Owlmen
If They See You, They Will Come for You

Ellie Blake is recovering from a nervous breakdown. Deciding to move back to her northern roots, she and her psychiatrist husband buy Tanners Dell at auction – an old water mill in the moorland village of Bridesmoor.

However, there is disquiet in the village. Tanners Dell has a terrible secret, one so well guarded no one speaks its name. But in her search for meaning and very much alone, Ellie is drawn to traditional witchcraft and determined to pursue it. All her life she has been cowed. All her life she has apologised for her very existence. And witchcraft has opened a door she could never have imagined. Imbued with power and overawed with its magic, for the first time she feels she has come home, truly knows who she is.

Tanners Dell, though, with its centuries-old demonic history…well, it's a dangerous place for a novice…

***

THE SOPRANO
A HAUNTING SUPERNATURAL THRILLER

It is 1951 and a remote mining village on the North Staffordshire Moors is hit by one of the worst snowstorms in living memory. Cut off for over three weeks, the old and the sick will die, the strongest bunker down, and those with evil intent will bring to its conclusion a family vendetta spanning three generations.

Inspired by a true event, The Soprano tells the story of Grace Holland – a strikingly beautiful, much admired local celebrity who brings glamour and inspiration to the grimy moorland community. But why is Grace still here? Why doesn't she leave this staunchly Methodist, rain-sodden place and the isolated farmhouse she shares with her mother?

Riddled with witchcraft and tales of superstition, the story is mostly narrated by the Whistler family, who own the local funeral parlour, in particular six-year-old Louise – now an elderly lady – who recalls one of the most shocking crimes imaginable.

***

Hidden Company
A dark psychological thriller set in a Victorian asylum in the heart of Wales.

1893, and nineteen-year-old Flora George is admitted to a remote asylum with no idea why she is there, what happened to her child, or how her wealthy family could have abandoned her to such a fate. However, within a short space of time, it becomes apparent she must save herself from something far worse than that of a harsh regime.

2018, and forty-one-year-old Isobel Lee moves into the gatehouse of what was once the old asylum. A reluctant medium, it is with dismay she realises there is a terrible secret here – one desperate to be heard. Angry and upset, Isobel baulks at what she must now face. But with the help of local dark arts practitioner Branwen, face it she must.

This is a dark story of human cruelty, folklore and superstition. But the human spirit can and Will prevail…unless of course, the wrath of the fae is incited…

***

MONKSPIKE
YOU ARE NOT FORGIVEN

1149 was a violent year in the Forest of Dean.

Today, nearly 900 years later, the forest village of Monkspike sits brooding. There is a sickness here passed down through ancient lines, one noted and deeply felt by Sylvia Massey, the new psychologist. What is wrong with Nurse Belinda Sully's son? Why did her husband take his own life? Why are the old people in Temple Lake Nursing Home so terrified? And what are the lawless inhabitants of nearby Wolfs Cross hiding?

It is a dark village indeed, but one which has kept its secrets well. That is, until local girl Kezia Elwyn returns home as a practising Satanist, and resurrects a hellish wrath no longer containable. Burdo, the white monk, will infest your dreams… This is pure occult horror and definitely not for the faint of heart…

***

BABA LENKA
PURE OCCULT HORROR

1970, and Baba Lenka begins in an icy Bavarian village with a highly unorthodox funeral. The deceased is Baba Lenka, great-grandmother to Eva Hart. But a terrible thing happens at the funeral, and from that moment on everything changes for seven year old Eva. The family flies back to Yorkshire but it seems the cold Alpine winds have followed them home...and the ghost of Baba Lenka has followed Eva. This is a story of demonic sorcery and occult practices during the World Wars, the horrors of which are drip-fed into young Eva's mind to devastating effect. Once again, this is absolutely not for the faint of heart. Nightmares pretty much guaranteed...

***

MASQUERADE
A BETH HARPER SUPERNATURAL THRILLER
BOOK 1

The first in a series of Beth Harper books, Masquerade is a supernatural thriller set in a remote North Yorkshire village. Following a whirlwind re-location for a live-in job at the local inn, Beth quickly realises the whole village is thoroughly haunted, the people here fearful and cowed. As a spiritual medium, her attention is drawn to Scarsdale Hall nearby, the enormous stately home dominating what is undoubtedly a wild and beautiful landscape. Built of black stone with majestic turrets, it seems to drain the energy from the land. There is, she feels, something malevolent about it, as if time has stopped...

***

CADUCEUS
BOOK TWO IN THE BETH HARPER SUPERNATURAL THRILLER SERIES.

'Beth Harper is a highly gifted spiritual medium and clairvoyant. Having fled Scarsdale Hall, she's drawn to the remote coastal town of Crewby in North West England, and it soon becomes apparent she has a job to do. The congeniality here is but a thin veneer masking decades of deeply embedded secrets, madness and fear. Although she has help from her spirit guides and many clues are shown in visions, it isn't until the senseless and ritualistic murders happen on Mailing Street, however, that the truth is finally unearthed. And Joe Sully, the investigating officer, is about to have the spiritual awakening of his life.

What's buried beneath these houses though, is far more horrific and widespread than anything either of them could have imagined. Who is the man in black? What is the black goo crawling all over the rooftops? What exactly is The Gatehouse? And as for the local hospital, one night is more than enough for Beth...let alone three...'

***

THE WITCHING HOUR
A COLLECTION OF THRILLERS, CHILLERS AND MYSTERIES

The title story, 'The Witching Hour' inspired the prologue for 'Father of Lies'. Other stories include, 'Someone out There,' a three part crime thriller set on the Yorkshire moorlands; 'The Witchfinders', a spooky 17th century witch hunt; and 'Cold Melon Tart,' where the waitress discovers there are some things she simply cannot do. In, 'A Second Opinion,' a consultant surgeon is haunted by his late mistress; and 'Sixty Seconds' sees a nursing home manager driven to murder. Whatever you choose, hopefully you'll enjoy the ride.

***

Printed in Great Britain
by Amazon